I Travel by
Night

ROBERT McCAMMON

SUBTERRANEAN PRESS • 2013

First Edition

ISBN
978-1-59606-537-6

Subterranean Press
PO Box 190106
Burton, MI 48519

www.subterraneanpress.com

One.

THE MAN WHO HAD COME to New Orleans on the afternoon train from Shreveport walked across the lobby of the Hotel Sanctuaire with a slow gait. He was carrying a heavy burden. From his high-backed chair in the shadowed corner Trevor Lawson smoked a thin black cheroot and watched him with slightly narrowed blue eyes, and he thought *Here is the man who needs me.*

David Kingsley, his name was. Of the Kingsley lumber family in Shreveport. Very wealthy, very powerful in Louisiana politics. But right now, at this moment in the evening of July 15th, 1886, David Kingsley had the slumped shoulders and bleary unfocused eyes of a weak pauper.

Lawson was surprised that the man had come alone. A quick glance around told him that indeed Kingsley—a slim man wearing a black suit, a white shirt with a bow tie and a black derby hat—had entered the red-carpeted lobby in a state of solitary submission to the power that bade him arrive here upon the hour of nine o'clock. It was time for the introduction. Lawson tapped ash from his Marsh-Wheeling cigar into the green glass ashtray on the table beside him and then rose to his full height of three inches over six feet.

"Mr. Kingsley," said Lawson, in a voice of gray gunsmoke and amber whiskey with a trace of Alabama wilderness, "I am here."

"Thank God!" the man said, upon seeing what he hoped was a light in the darkness. And Lawson just smiled slightly at this painful statement of thanks, and motioned for Kingsley to take the red-cushioned chair at his side.

In the rainwashed city of New Orleans the gas lamps hissed, the barkeeps offered exotic drinks from potion bottles of many colors, the restaurants served Creole and Cajun fare that put heat into the stomach, blood and loins, sweet ladies paraded and posed before young gentlemen seeking an evening of delight, laughter rose up from shadows and then fell back into darkness again, horse-drawn carriages moved here and there in no particular hurry as if the night had no beginning nor end, guitar and piano music spilled into the puddled streets from rooms made golden by candlelight, the timeless river washed against the piers and pilings of exquisite decay, and the brick walls that had stood in the reign of the Ibervilles still stood in defiance of sun, wind, the dampness of the swamp and the hands of modern men. It was a magic and mystical city, wild in its freedoms and sacred in its charms. Yet for David Kingsley and the man named Lawson, it was a place for an urgent and hushed conversation, because a young woman's life hung in the balance.

Kingsley removed his derby. His hair was dark brown and going gray on the sides, and gray flecked his mustache. He took his seat, looked nervously around the lobby at the few other people there engaged in quiet talk, and he cleared his throat as if to speak but did not speak. Lawson sat down and waited. He calmly smoked his cheroot. If Lawson had learned anything in the past number of years, it was how to remain still and silent. His blue eyes were intense and clear. His steady gaze conveyed both self-control and the keenest edge of danger. He was lean and rawboned and appeared to be about thirty, but age mattered nothing to him now. He had blonde hair combed back from the high forehead and left shaggy at the neck. He was clean-shaven; one interesting effect of his condition was that he no longer had to shave. Another was that he could throw his Eye into a human head to read the secrets there, though often they were only shadows of things that used to be, and misshapen moments that lived in the soul like deformed dreams, difficult to decipher.

He wore black trousers, a cream-colored jacket, a pale blue shirt, a darker blue cravat and a waistcoat decorated in a pattern of blue and gray paisleys. On his feet were ordinary black boots, scuffed by hard circumstances. To his left, hanging on a hook beneath a painting of an ivy-covered Vieux Carré wall, was his black felt Stetson hat with a cattleman's crease. It sported a thin band made from rattlesnake scales. This night he wasn't wearing his gunbelt, but close at hand on the left side beneath his jacket was a double-barrelled Remington Model 95 derringer with a mother-of-pearl grip, just in case of particular difficulty.

"Tell me," said Lawson, as he exhaled a plume of smoke. Through the haze his eyes were watchful. He had received a letter from David Kingsley two weeks ago, had digested that as best he could, and sent back his business card. On the plain white card, beneath his name and the address of the Hotel Sanctuaire, was the line *All Matters Handled*. And below that: *I Travel By Night*.

Kingsley nodded. He looked dazed, in need of more than just a listener. "I'd like a whiskey," he managed to say.

Lawson raised his hand to get the attention of Tolliver, one of the Negro waiters who tended to the lobby. Kingsley ordered a straight shot of whiskey and Lawson asked for his usual drink of rye, simple syrup and orange bitters. Tolliver went off to the bar, and Lawson continued to smoke his cigar and wait for the story.

Kingsley shifted in his chair. There was no need for Lawson to send his Eye out; the man was ready to talk. "As I said in my letter...I received a...certain message after my daughter was taken. Here it is." He reached into his coat and brought out a folded piece of paper, dark-stained and mottled. It appeared to be more lizard skin than paper. Lawson accepted it from Kingley's hand, opened it, and read what was written there in elegant penmanship:

Your daughter is very beautiful, Mr. Kingsley. Very charming indeed. And worth money to you, I'm sure. She is being well-looked after. To return her to you, I require gold pieces in the amount of six hundred and sixty-six dollars. She is being held in the town of Nocturne, which is reached from the hamlet of St. Benadicta. It will not be on the map. If you try to bring authorities into this matter, I fear your lovely Eva will come to some harm. Therefore my instructions to you are these: Inform only one man of this, and send him to me with the gold. His name is Trevor Lawson and he resides in the Hotel Sanctuaire on Conti Street in New Orleans. He is what you might call an 'adventurer'. Send him to me, Mr. Kingsley, and your daughter shall be released unharmed but perhaps wiser to the ways of the world. I shall expect to welcome Mr. Lawson before July has ended.

The letter was signed, with a flourish: *Yours Truly, Christian Melchoir.*

"I see," said Lawson. He refolded the paper and ran his fingers across the texture. The stains had been made by dirty water. Swamp water, most likely. He was sure he would find on the map of Louisiana that St. Benadicta was a small town whose fishing wharves fell off to the muddy unknown. And Nocturne? Oh yes…the music of the night.

Tolliver brought their drinks on a black lacquered tray. Lawson tipped him a silver dollar. When Tolliver left them, Lawson took a small red bottle from the inside of his coat, uncorked it and poured a spool of thick, crimson liquid into his drink. "My extra ingredient," he said to Kingley's curious appraisal, but he said no more. He recorked the bottle, put it away and clinked his glass against the other man's. "To the business at hand," Lawson offered, "and to a successful conclusion."

"God help my daughter," said Kingsley, as he downed the shot.

"God may not be in this lobby tonight," Lawson answered, after he had taken a sip of his elixir. "But I hope I will do." He swirled the drink around in the glass and watched the crimson form sinuous shapes. "Do you know the name Christian Melchoir?"

"No. Do you?"

"I do not. However, he seems to know me." Of course they had spies everywhere. They knew where he was, that was no stretch of the imagination. "You said in your letter that your daughter was taken on her way to the theater? She was alone in her carriage, I believe you said?"

"Yes, that's correct."

"And the abduction was after dusk?"

"Yes, the sheriff thinks it happened around eight o'clock. Eva was running late. She was supposed to meet two friends in front of the *Armitage*."

"The sheriff doesn't know about your communication from Christian Melchoir?"

"No. From what it said…I didn't dare."

"Hm." Lawson took another drink of his ruddy fortification. "For the best, I think. I have no doubt Miss Eva might be…shall we say…in grave circumstances if these instructions aren't obeyed."

"I don't fathom this." Kingsley stared at the floor for a moment, and Lawson could guess what the man was going to say when he spoke again. "You know…I would think it very peculiar, my daughter being taken by this bastard—whoever he is—and then writing me to request *you* bring the ransom money. And why six hundred and sixty-six dollars in gold? I am presuming you require a not insubstantial fee?"

"My fee will be two thousand dollars," Lawson replied.

"Ah. So you might understand how...excuse me for thinking this...you might be involved somewhat more in this situation?"

"I do understand." Lawson let that sit for a few seconds, while he sipped his drink and then drew again on his cigar. He blew smoke toward the gas-lit chandelier at the ceiling. "I can tell you, sir," he continued with a calm stare into Kingsley's eyes, "that I know nothing of your daughter's kidnapping...except to say that this Christian Melchoir wants *me*, and is using your Eva as a device. Now...I could say I wouldn't go to Nocturne—wherever that is—and deliver this ransom for you, and I would be free not to deliver myself to whatever is waiting. I would think that might be the safest decision for myself. I suspect you would never see your daughter again. But," he shrugged, "I am perhaps what this letter suggests. An adventurer. Also I have a great curiosity, and like all of us I have bills to pay. I will tell you also...that I *will* go and deliver this ransom for you, and I will do my best to return your daughter in a whole state." It occurred to Lawson that one could never fully return to a whole state after exposure to the Dark Society, but he couldn't yet present that to Kingsley. "I'm presuming you have the portrait of Eva I asked you to bring?" He waited for Kingsley to nod. "Then if you'll also bring the gold pieces and leave them at the desk in the morning, I'll pick them up and be on my way tomorrow at nightfall."

"Very well." Kingsley still looked stunned, as was his right for a man whose nineteen-year-old daughter, the younger of his two, had been stolen away en route to a Shreveport theater. "I have to ask, though...what do you mean, this man wants *you*? And you say you don't know *him*?"

"I know his kind," was the reply.

"What would that be?"

"Evil to the bone," said Lawson. "Go back to your hotel and rest. You look as if you need it. Bring the items I've asked for. Then catch the train for home. You can pay me when I've returned Eva to you."

"Don't you want at least half your payment?"

"No." It was not worth saying that if he didn't return from Nocturne, the money would be useless to him. He stood up, took his Stetson hat from the wallpeg and put it on. He finished his drink with a final swallow. "I'll walk you out, sir."

On Conti Street, the wet night air smelled of sassafras and coffee. Across the way, Sam Bordine's coffee shop was in full operation, roasting beans on the premises. Carriages trundled back and forth. Candles showed in windows above the street, and figures stood on balconies watching what was to be seen. Lawson stood with Kingsley under the red awning over the Sanctuaire's entrance, surveying the passage of people, horses and carriages.

"Thank you," said Kingsley, reaching out to shake Lawson's hand. Lawson took the offered hand and saw Kingsley wince just a little. The night was warm, but Lawson's hand was cold. Lawson released the grip as fast as he could without being rude. "Maybe I shouldn't agree to this," Kingsley added, as he stood unconsciously rubbing the hand that had just been affected with a chill. "But do I have a choice?"

"You do not," Lawson said, which was the truth.

Kingsley nodded. Lawson drew on his cheroot once more, blew a smoke ring into the air and surveyed the street. He caught the quickest glimpse of a figure on the right, pulling itself back around the corner of Conti and Royal streets; he had registered a tall, thin man in a black tophat and long black duster, the man's face indistinct.

"Tell me this," Kingsley ventured, his expression a mix of personal pain and professional puzzlement. "About your business card. Why does it say, 'I Travel By Night'?"

"My habit," was the measured response. Lawson's gaze swept past the corner and again caught the merest shape of a face under a tophat, leaning forward and now quickly pulling back once more. "I have a skin condition that prevents me from enjoying sunlight. It's been many years since I've been afflicted." He smiled faintly behind his veil of smoke, aware that he was extraordinarily pale for a rugged-looking man and that a tracery of blue veins showed at his temples. "Unfortunately," he said, "the cure is...somewhat distant."

"I'm sorry," the other man offered, and now it was clear he had decided he must be on his way, either because he had to trust his daughter's life to a man he hardly knew or that the cold touch of Trevor Lawson's hand was slowly moving up his forearm. "Well then... I'll say goodnight, sir. What you require will be brought to the front desk in the morning." He paused on the edge of walking away. "I don't understand this business with Christian Melchoir or why it involves you and my Eva, but...I thank you for helping me."

"My pleasure," Lawson answered, and thought *My fate.*

David Kingsley walked on. He turned to the left, going to the northeast on Royal. Lawson spent a moment striking a friction match and relighting a cheroot that had never gone out, the better to watch from behind a cupped hand as the tall thin man in the black tophat and duster left his place of concealment and strode after the departing Kingsley, firing a single quick glance at Lawson before he moved out of sight.

So, Lawson thought as he smoked, *their spy is in pursuit. Then I shall also go in pursuit,* he decided, *and I will see what this spy is made of.*

He walked to the corner of Conti and Royal and turned left, walking neither too fast nor too slowly, just ambling along. He passed beneath the yellow glow of a gas lamp, which revealed upon his pallid face the thin-lipped smile of a predator.

TWO.

TREVOR LAWSON SAW THE TWO men ahead
on Royal Street. First the top-hatted stalker and then
David Kingsley, derby-hatted and freighted down with
his burden of worry. The stalker was following Kingsley
to his hotel, which Lawson knew from a previous letter
was the very luxurious St. Roman on Dumaine Street.
Lawson figured the stalker might be also going to report
to someone else that the meeting between Kingsley and
himself had taken place, and thus in time the unknown
Christian Melchoir would know that 'the adventurer'
was on his way.

Lawson realized of course what he was walking into. He knew what they wanted. But if it meant

finding out *anything* about LaRouge...then it was a risk worth taking.

The problem was not getting into Nocturne. Oh no, they would welcome him there. The problem would be in getting out.

As they said in Alabama, his home state, *if you're gonna jump into that fryin' pan, make sure you're plenty oiled up.*

He intended to be.

He kept himself at a leisurely pace. The stalker had long legs, but was also holding himself back as not to get too close to Kingsley's shadow as thrown by Royal's ornate green gaslamps. As they strolled deeper into the Vieux Carré, the traffic of pedestrians and carriages dwindled. The St. Roman was only a block ahead. Lawson had smoked his cheroot down to its nub, and now he paused to flick it into a puddle of rainwater. The hiss that followed—as soft as it was—made Kingsley's stalker suddenly look back over his shoulder. Lawson saw the deep-sunken eyes glint. The man darted away onto St. Ann Street in a black swirl, heading northwest toward Dauphine.

Ah! Lawson thought, with a measure of satisfaction. *He wants a chase!* Being a gentleman, Lawson could not refuse such an invitation. He tied the leather chinstrap of his hat into place, for he'd lost valuable Stetsons before and this one suited him very well.

He propelled himself forward and turned onto St. Ann. How this was done was child's play to him, but to anyone else he would have appeared a phantom figure in a blur of clothing, passing by like a cool breeze with breathtaking speed. He was not running, nor was he expending a great amount of energy; he was moving with the night, as part of the currents of the night, and using the power that had been given to him by the woman—the creature—he so desperately sought.

He would go to the ends of the earth to find LaRouge. He would assault the gates of Hell itself to get at her, for he knew that territory very intimately. He had lived there, since the month of April in the year of 1862.

But for now, he was determined not to let his quarry slip away...for the man ahead was also a phantom figure in a blur of clothing, but Lawson's eyes—red-centered now, and shining like a cat's—marked the stalker's progress as if they were still strolling, as if other passersby were frozen in place like so many full-sized daguerreotype photographs.

Lawson saw the man turn swiftly to the right upon Bourbon Street, one hand up to hold the tophat from flying off his head. Lawson kept pace, a blur following a shadow. They crossed Bourbon and turned left onto Dumaine. At the corner they frightened a carriage horse that snorted and reared and made the already-besotted driver think he'd caught a quick glimpse of French Quarter specters that called for another cup of rum.

Halfway between Dumaine and Burgundy, where patterns of ivy decorated yellow walls and lamps of many colors flickered in garret windows, the top-hatted man suddenly turned to his right and leaped a seven-foot-tall wrought-iron gate with speartips at the top. It was done smoothly and soundlessly, but a gray cat saw it and, scrowling, scrambled for the cover of a maidenhair fern. Lawson reached the gate within three seconds. A courtyard lay beyond with a fountain at its center. There was a scrabbling noise from above, and Lawson's red-centered eyes caught sight of the top-hatted man climbing up over a balcony twenty feet above the courtyard and then springing up like a spider to catch the roof's gutter and pull himself over the edge. By that time, Lawson was already going over the gate in a smooth leap of his own. He sometimes snagged clothing doing this, leaving tatters of shirts or—more regrettably, bits of trousers—left behind, for no one was perfect all the time...but in this case he came over the speartips into the courtyard still fully clothed, and next he sprang up off the bricks to grasp hold of the balcony's railing and haul himself over. A small dog began to bark furiously beyond the window curtains. Lawson was already going up onto the roof, and crouching there to smell the air for the friction of movement.

He had not been born this way. No one was. It was lost in the mists of time who the first one had been and what agreement had spawned such a condition, but now they were legion. It had occurred to Lawson on many occasions just such as this, when all his senses quivered on the alert, the black ichor burned in his veins and his eyes saw through the dark as if they themselves were spirit lamps, that he had never felt more alive. As a lover of the night, he caressed with his senses the sinuous dark. He had been torn apart as a man in 1862 and reformed as something both more and less. He had no choice about what he was; his choice lay in what he was to do with himself, and in what he sought. But even in his darkest moments, when he felt so distant from humanity and so lonely for a warm touch that he might scream to wake the dead, he had to think that this was a gift. Sent from Satan, yes...but indeed, a *gift*.

He wished to return it to its sender, as the riverboat gamblers might say..."in spades".

He looked out across the sea of roofs beneath the vault of stars, where the last of the surly rainclouds were drifting into tatters. There was no sight of the top-hatted stalker, in among the sharp peaks and edges and the multiple chimneys. But Lawson knew he must be here somewhere, for the spy had brought Lawson up to this high place for them to be alone. Lawson figured the man intended to kill him. It was a matter of pride for some.

Lawson moved forward, cautiously and carefully, along a roof's peak. A carriage passed by on Dumaine Street about sixty feet beneath him, the horse's hooves clip-clopping on the cobbles. Somewhere below, a bottle shattered. Lawson wished he had something to drink, and not just the little weak "tea" from his Japanese bottle that had once held the ashes of a warlord's heart. No, tonight he desired the stronger elixir.

He had crossed the apex of one roof and was continuing across a second, past a pair of darkened garret windows in the shape of diamonds, when a figure rose up from behind a red brick chimney to his right.

Lawson stopped his advance. The tall thin man in the top hat stood staring at him, a faint breeze stirring the folds of the man's ebony duster. Lawson caught the red centers of the man's eyes; they were brothers, of a fashion.

"I suppose you know me," said Lawson, his voice easy.

The stalker did not speak for a few long seconds. Then, in a rasp as if from a parched throat: "I know you. What you are. And I will tell you that Christian Melchoir will reward me very well for your death."

"Your reward, sir," answered the vampire in the Stetson hat, "will be delivered to you in Hell."

The other removed his top hat to reveal slicked-back black hair and an elongated and strangely pointed head. When he grinned, the fangs slid out like those of

a rattlesnake. "You may go first, sir," he hissed, "and pre-pare the way."

So saying, he revealed himself further. He was still grinning as his legs and arms lengthened and thinned and the black duster flew away from the changing body like the wings of a raven. The flesh darkened to the color of a bruise in the space of several seconds. There was the noise of bones cracking and reshaping. Ripples of pain shot across the shapechanger's damp face because nothing in this world—or even the world to which this creature belonged—was born in the absence of agony. The features flattened, the chest bulged and grew large as an armor plate, the hands became dark-nailed claws and the feet on the ends of the grotesque spidery legs stepped out of their boots. The face was still barely human, the red-centered eyes narrowed to slits. As the body shook off its trousers and shirt and black silk ascot and became yet more spider-like the lower jaw unhinged and thrust forward and the vampiric fangs in the upper jaw snapped and tore at the air.

By instinct Lawson's own face tightened, his mouth opened and the fangs slid out. He was already reaching in a blur for the derringer beneath his jacket. He brought the gun out and cocked the hammer, and just that fast the man-spider scrabbled forward and a dark forelimb stubbled with spiky growths whipped out. It caught Lawson's forearm and knocked the weapon aside just as the derringer fired. Trailing blue flame, the bullet shot away toward the stars.

And then the nightmare was upon him.

It enveloped him with its foreclaws and, gripping him around the back, lifted him up off the roof. The fanged mouth in the misshapen face came at Lawson's throat, going for the ichor that gave life to death; Lawson got his left elbow up and slammed it against the creature's jaw with a force that would have broken the neck of an ordinary human, but this was a member of the Dark Society and so was both far beyond and far beneath humanity. Still, the man-spider blinked and fell back, stunned. A claw shifted position and grasped the wrist of Lawson's gunhand before he could put the weapon to action again. Lawson's arm was trapped by tremendous strength, his body still lifted into the air, and with his other fist he struck desperately into the creature's face with all the power given him by the Devil's brood.

It was not enough.

Though Lawson was a creature of the night himself, and some might—certainly *would*...say he was a monster, he was still human enough to possess organs and bones, and these could be ruptured and broken. He would not be killed in this way, but the pain would be fierce and he would be debilitated for a time until everything healed together again. He was hard to kill, but he was not invulnerable. He was aware of this as his body was squeezed by the thing's other spidery foreclaw and he felt the vertebrae of his spine pop. He felt the pressure at his ribs and at his chest. He took a breath of the heated air between himself and the monster and held it. The head darted forward again, the fangs questing for his throat. Lawson kicked into the monster's midsection with a force that would've knocked a carriage onto its side, interrupting that particular attempt to draw ichor. The man-spider staggered back to the edge of the roof above Dumaine but still wouldn't let Lawson go. He kicked into its midsection once more, like kicking into a chunk of concrete. They danced back and forth atop the roof in a macabre roundabout. Lawson heard the Japanese bottle in his coat pocket shatter. Wetness spread. The smell of blood was overpowering, a heady incense, and for an instant the man-spider blinked and its hold on Lawson's gunhand faltered.

Lawson cocked the derringer, held its barrel against the thing's dark forehead and pulled the trigger.

The creature's head snapped back, its jaws opened and the rattlesnake vampiric fangs were exposed in all their gleaming glory. But Trevor Lawson knew they would not be tasting blood—or in his case, ichor—ever again.

Still, the man-spider didn't fully understand yet. Its strength was still undiminished. The narrow red-centered eyes stared at him with something akin to humor and ablaze with hatred. Then the head began to swell and the face to warp, and one of the eyes imploded and went black like a dying comet. The open mouth gasped around the fangs, which began to turn the color of cinders.

The creature's grip loosened enough for Lawson to fight free. He dropped to the roof, thinking that if anyone was in the room below they had gotten a noise like a drum parade over their heads. He crawled up to the roof's apex and sat there, watching the creature shiver and writhe and begin to crack apart like old pottery. Cracks rippled across the agonized face and crisscrossed the chest. Between the cracks glowed a pulsing red heat like a glimpse beyond the iron gates of Hell. The monster held its claws before the fissured face, as the single eye sought to fathom what was happening; the left claw was already falling apart in whorls of gray ashes. The remaining eye went dark. With a high-pitched shriek that was no longer the sound of any human being, the dissolving man-spider scrabbled toward Lawson as if to take a last bite of revenge, but its knotty legs were coming apart. Lawson kicked the thing in the chest as it reached him.

It staggered backward, and backward again, and as it flailed at the air it fell from the rooftop and, falling toward the stones of Dumaine Street, it cracked into dozens of small pieces. There was a fall of ugly gray ash upon Dumaine. All that remained for the streetsweeper to find and wonder about was the pair of black socks that lay mysteriously full of ashes.

Lawson pulled a few deep breaths into lungs that were losing their power to draw air. He put the empty derringer away and removed a cheroot from the inside of his coat. He found it half-crushed. Tearing it in two, he threw the crushed half aside and lit the survivor with a friction match. He sat and blew smoke rings and listened to dogs howling in the aftermath of the creature's eerie shriek. He decided it wouldn't do to sit here too long. Some of the windows would surely be opening soon. It was time to descend into the shadows, his home away from home.

Lawson got up. His vertebrae popped back into place; it was a good feeling. His chest felt a little smashed and the muscles of both shoulders throbbed, but he was all right. His cream-colored jacket, however, was a bloody disaster from the broken Japanese bottle, which had cost him a pretty gold piece from a Royal Street antiques vendor. *Damn*, he thought. But what he was trying to do was keep his mind from the fact that he'd never seen a member of the Dark Society quite like that one before, and it was more than a little disturbing to realize how their shapechanging was becoming so...the word would be *advanced*. Then with the cigar between his teeth and his fangs back in their sockets where polite vampire gentlemen kept theirs, Lawson took a first step and nearly fell on his southern comfort. He had to get his balance and his focus back before he went any further. It took him a minute or so. He had somewhere to be, and continuing across the roof to find the nearest balcony and the easiest way down he left puffs of smoke behind him like the trail of ghosts that haunted his memory.

Three.

WHEN LAWSON REACHED THE WOODEN gate that had an image of a kneeling Jesus carved upon it, his mouth was bloody. The blood had run down his chin; he'd used a handkerchief to try to clean up, but it was useless. His willpower was going. It was a battle he had fought long and hard, every day of this cursed life, but he knew that—like Shiloh in that Bloody April—it was a battle he was bound to lose.

The gate was unlocked, and opened onto a stone path that led through a garden. Crickets chirped in the grass and other insects whirred and sang softly in the trees. It was a place of peace, but there was no peace in what remained the human part of Trevor Lawson's soul.

He followed the path past a white-painted church with a steeple and belltower and then to a small house next to the church, where he walked up upon the darkened front porch and pulled a cord that rang a little silver bell within. He waited, smelling the blood that stained him. His stomach lurched, but his veins sang. In another moment gas lamps came on inside the house, showing through the windows, and a figure in a dark blue robe with a red sash approached the door. The figure held a pair of tapers in a candleholder. When the door was opened, the candleglow fell upon Lawson's gore-smeared face.

"Oh," said the elderly man, with a pained frown. His hair was a white cloud, his face deeply wrinkled, his chin wide and square and his nose a magnificent statement of God's ability to create an oversized monument out of flesh. "I'm suspecting that's not blood from a cow, is it?"

Lawson shook his head.

"Come in," said the man. "Don't drip."

"It's mostly dried." Lawson answered, as he crossed the threshold. The door was closed behind him. Lawson stood in a comfortable sitting-room with several over-stuffed chairs and a brown sofa. Above a fireplace was hung a white crucifix, the sight of which made Lawson's eyes burn and water, so he chose to look away. That, too, was getting worse.

"You," said Father John Deale, "look a mess." He sighed heavily. "We'll get you cleaned up, but...oh Lord, your jacket. Ruined, of course. Do I dare to ask...*who* supplied your meal tonight?"

Lawson took his Stetson off. He ran a hand through his shaggy blonde hair. He felt a hundred years old, but in truth he was only fifty two. Though he appeared to be nearer thirty, his age before his rebirth had been twenty-seven. "There was a drunkard lying in a doorway on Dauphine Street," he said, his gaze cast to the smooth-planked floor. "A middle-aged man, sleeping. I wanted to walk past. I *tried*."

"Not very successfully, I see," said Father Deale, setting the candleholder on a sidetable.

"No, not very." Lawson hung his hat upon a wall rack. His eyes were flinty. "He just...was *there*, and he smelled of bourbon and cigar smoke, and his blood was fresh. I did try to walk past, but..." His gaze, imploring, went to the priest. "Yes, I nearly killed him. Dragged him into an alley and drained him almost dry, so that *I* could live. And that's my story, isn't it?"

"For now. But you have the power to write a new one."

"With red ink?" asked Lawson. His bloody smile would have terrified anyone in New Orleans, but Father Deale knew him. Father Deale supported Lawson as he could, for Lawson in spite of all appearances was on the side of the angels.

"Blue ink, in time. With a regular pen and not...
these." The priest waved an age-spotted hand in front of
his own mouth, indicating the eye teeth. Of which his
were entirely normal. "Come into the bathroom, let's get
your mess cleaned up."

When the job was done, the blood wiped away and
Lawson's jacket and shirt removed and replaced by an
indigo shirt from Father Deale's closet, the priest guided
Lawson back to the sitting room. He poured Lawson a glass
of Medoc, and himself the same. Lawson sank into a chair,
recalling the first time he had staggered to this man's door
nearly two years ago, in a similar bloodied condition, to fall
upon his knees and beg for forgiveness. The priest had listened in silence to the vampire's story, and at last had given
him a prayer not only of forgiveness but also of strength.
And thus had their friendship—and partnership, in a
way—begun, as Father Deale had become Lawson's con-
nection to the daytime world, his support in tribulations
like this one, and his hope that one day he might throw off
this heavy burden and find his way back to the sun.

But to do that, Lawson would have to find—and
kill—the vampire he knew as LaRouge. There had been
many trails, but always she slipped the moment. The
Dark Society protected her, for she was their deathless
and beautiful Queen.

"Christian Melchoir," said Lawson, after a few sips of
the Medoc. "Whoever he is, he knows me. He has a young

woman in a swamp town called Nocturne. Kidnapped her. I'm to deliver the ransom."

"A trap, of course." The priest had situated himself in another chair across from his visitor.

"I HAVE TO go. Into what…I don't know. But I have to." Lawson drank from his glass again. It wasn't the exlixir of life for him but it was a very good substitute, just as were the bottles of cattle blood that Father Deale supplied to him from the slaughterhouse in Algiers across the river. *For religious purposes*, the priest told the slaughterhouse manager. Nobody asked any questions, the blood was bought and paid for. Cattle blood served its purpose of keeping Lawson alive, but after a time of that he found his senses dulled and his appetite for the human substance as demanding as the need for any opiate, yet the drinking of human blood awakened his senses to their fullest. The longest he'd ever gone without opening a human vein was three months, which had reduced him nearly to a hobbling husk.

"Will you come out of there, is the question," said Father Deale, with a lifting of his thick white eyebrows. "And you know the Dark Society will never let a human woman go free. She's likely already been turned."

"Possibly." Lawson saw some blood under the fingernails of his left hand that the washcloth had missed. Now that he was full, the sight was repellent. He closed the hand into a fist. The priest's understanding of the Dark Society was not just through Lawson's experience. He had had his own encounter with otherworldly forces when he was a younger man, in the now-forgotten town of Blancmortain, in western Louisiana. Over the long hot summer of 1838, John Deale had been witness to the deaths of ten townspeople due to snakelike bites on the throat and the draining of blood. That had caused the citizens of the little farming community to panic and pack up, leaving Blancmortain for whatever force wished to live there.

"Something happened tonight," Lawson went on. "I know I almost murdered someone. That's not what I mean. I had...an encounter with something. A vampire, yes...but *more*. I've seen shapechangers before, but never one like that." He took one more drink and set the glass aside. Across the room, a pendulum clock chimed the hour of two. "I think as they age, they become more adept at it. I think...something of their spirit...their essence... is involved. This one...was very strong. If I hadn't had the bullets...well, thank God—and *you*—for those."

"Pleased to do my part. How are you set?"

"I'm fine with the Colt, but I'll need a box more for the derringer."

"All right. You're leaving on this mission soon?"

"Tomorrow night." Lawson glanced at the hands on the clock. "*Tonight*, I mean."

"What you need will be ready for you by sundown. Shall I have it sent to the hotel?"

Lawson nodded. That was the usual arrangement.

"Is there anything else I can help you with?"

Lawson thought about it. He looked at the crucifix above the mantel, and again his eyes watered and burned. He had not been very religious before his conversion, but now he longed for the healing touch and mercy of God yet he felt so distant from it. He considered that this feeling grew stronger in the vampire tribe until it became pure rage toward anything Good in this universe. He pulled his gaze away from the Cross. "I may need," said Lawson after another moment, "something else. Let me think. I'm going walking in awhile, by the river. I'll write you what I need before dawn and have the note sent to you in the morning."

"All right. I'll do what I can."

That was all Lawson could ask. Both of them knew he might not come back from this nest of the Dark Society called Nocturne. But both of them also knew he had no choice but to go.

He stood up and retrieved his black Stetson. "Thank you, Father," he said quietly. "As always...your help is much appreciated. I'll leave you now."

Father Deale stood up as well. He reached out and touched Lawson's shoulder, then drew his hand back because the vampire in the room had flinched slightly. "You're in pain?"

"Bruises," said Lawson. He smiled grimly. "But yes… always in pain." He waited for the priest to open the door. He took one more look at the crucifix, held it as long as he could, and then looked away. "Thank you, John," he said.

"I'll pray for you."

"Pray for a young woman named Eva Kingsley," Lawson answered, putting the Stetson on his head. "Pray for her soul and her sanity. Good morning to you." He started to go out, but a thought—a question—occurred to him that caused him to hesitate. He frowned, staring into the priest's dark brown eyes. "Do you think I'm the only one who fights back?"

Father Deale took a moment in replying. "I think," he said, "you're the only one who fights back who has survived so long. That's why they so desperately want you destroyed." Lawson went out the door, onto the path that led through the garden, and into the night.

He walked at a human pace, a solitary figure no longer absolutely human.

The night was his territory, his world, his blessing. It was also his grief and his prison. Away from the glare of the sun that hurt the eyes and burned the flesh, he was aware of the perfume of the night breezes, the stillness of the dark, the protection he enjoyed between the hours of dawn and dusk. This was his time, yet he longed to walk in the daylight and to witness the sun's movement. How he missed the shadows of midday! His flesh could not bear such fierce fire, even on a cloudy day. His rhythm and habits now were dictated by the creature within, the monster that LaRouge had created. He was a construction still of heart and lungs, of bone and muscle. Yet he felt his humanity drifting away from him, night after night. When he drew the black curtains shut across the windows of his suite at the Hotel Sanctuaire and lay in the bed that was also draped with black curtains, he thought he might as well be positioning himself in a grave. He was always cold. He could never fully rest. Some part of himself reviled the other. He was caught in the midst of transformation, knowing that over time he would lose all his humanity and become a creature of blood need, not caring who he had to slaughter to get it. His body was changing; the strength and quickness were welcome attributes, yes, but it was in small things that he realized he was on a certain path to becoming a monster. He could still drink a little wine and liquor, but straight water made him sick. He peed maybe a shot glass full of murky brown liquid every few days. Food turned his stomach. He would never have believed, in his previous life, that he could have tracked his progress from man through the deepening clutches of vampirism by how little he pulled the chain on his toilet.

He was dying, of course. Becoming one of them, totally and truely, was a death in life. But he couldn't give up; he couldn't lie down in that grave and let *them* win. It was not in the nature of a captain of the Nineteenth Alabama Infantry Regiment, who had both taken blood and shed blood at the battle of Shiloh. It was not in the nature of Trevor Lawson, once a young Alabama lawyer and a valued husband and father.

He walked the night. He walked along the curve of the Mississippi. He walked through the silent streets of early morning, as he pondered the future. By the time he returned to the Hotel Sanctuaire, went to the front desk and wrote Garrison, the night clerk, a note to be delivered to Father John Deale at the Church of the Apostle St. Simon, the sun was a faint blush in the eastern sky. Lawson stood outside as long as he could, watching the light strengthen. Then he pulled his hat down low over his eyes and went up the stairs to his room, where he double-locked the door, closed the heavy black window curtains, took off his clothes and settled his pale naked body upon the bed. His bruises would fade quickly; they always did. He drew the black curtains around the bed and by habit touched the ebony leather-tooled gunbelt with the two backward-holstered Colt .44s that lay next to his right side. Now he could sleep.

Before he drifted off into dreams of again walking in the hot summer sun, his shadow striding in front of him like a taunt, Lawson heard the first of the street-vendors down on Conti Street begin their distinctive morning calls. It was a woman, calling in a musical sing-song voice, *"Apples, sweet apples, apples for sale."*

Lawson reluctantly let go of his hold on the daytime world. He sank away, in his soft grave beyond the curtains black.

Four.

ON THE ROAD TO ST. Benadicta, astride his muscular chestnut horse Phoenix, Lawson listened to the sounds of the night and warily scanned the forest beneath the brim of his black Stetson.

He wore a black suit, a white shirt and a crimson waistcoat. At his waist was the ebony holster with the two backward-facing Colt .44s. The Colt on the right had a rosewood grip and the Colt on the left had a grip formed of yellowed bone. Each pistol held six slugs. The gun on the right side held regular lead bullets, while the one on the left did not.

The moon was a white scythe above the treetops. Phoenix moved at a brisk walk. Lawson figured another couple of hours to St. Benadicta. If his estimation of speed and distance was correct, he would be beating daybreak by about an hour. There would be the problem of shelter; there always was that problem, but Lawson had solved it many times before. In his saddlebags were two folded-up black curtains, thick enough to wrap himself up in and have a comfortable outdoor sleep if he could find a suitable slice of shadow that didn't move too much. Usually there was a room available, for enough money. And he never slept like the dead anyway; if anyone burst the lock and got into his room with evil intent, even in midday, they wouldn't be leaving the same way they'd entered .

He listened to the churrings and clicks and rustlings of the nighttime forest, as Phoenix continued along the trail leading southwest into the bayou country. Lawson was alert but relaxed; he was confident in his ability to survive, yet he knew not to push his luck.

He had what he needed. Father Deale had been resourceful. Now it was up to Lawson to see things through. Tonight, before he'd left New Orleans, he'd had a further insight into the priest's desire to help him. A letter had come to the Hotel Sanctuaire with the requested package.

Lawson, the letter had begun in smoothly flowing blue handwriting. *I expect you'll find good use for these. I hope you'll return in one piece, along with the young woman. God protect her soul, I pray she's survived. I wanted to tell you that I consider it an act of God that you came to me in confession that night. I've told you about my time in Blancmortain, when I was married and a teacher in the school there. I've told you about the people who were found dead in that summer of 1838, drained of blood with the fang bites at their throats. What I've not told you, and what I choose to tell you now, is that in addition to the ten who were murdered in that fashion, four others disappeared. Among them was my wife, Emily. She came home one night at the end of that summer, Lawson. She came to my window, and she begged to come in because she was so cold. I almost let her in…almost. She was a wretched sight, half-naked, dirty and blighted and her face dark with dried blood. By that time they were feasting on other towns. By that time I knew what she was…what she'd been turned to. When I refused to let her in, Emily cursed me. No demon could voice the curses she threw at me. No horror could be more horrible than that, because Emily had been pregnant with our child and now she was a thin, ragged nightmare. It went on and on, until the sun came up. I packed and left that day. I am a different man now, because some of the man I used to be stayed in Blancmortain, holding hard to a crucifix he took off the wall. He is suffering there still, in that little house where no one dares live.*

I know what used to be my Emily is still out upon the world. She may be with the others in Nocturne, or she may be in another town far from there, living like an animal and a monster. But I have hope for you, Lawson, and if I have hope for you I also can find some hope for Emily. That she can come back to me, as she was before? Hardly. She will always be twenty years old. Isn't that the most terrible joke, Lawson? That if survives on blood, she will always be young? My hope for you is that you can find your way back to humanity. My hope for her is that she can be released from that existence, and die in the grace of God. I want you to release her if you find her, Lawson. If you can. I want you to do this for me, and for her. You do the mercy, and I will take care of the grace. For all three of us, suffering as we are.

God be with you, Lawson. I know you travel by night. He does too.

And the missive was signed, Your friend, John.

Phoenix went on. The moon moved across the sky. The forest pulsed with life unseen, though Lawson caught the occasional shape of an animal out in the dark. The ground was still firm, not yet swampy. Above his head the canopy of trees blotted out the stars. Lawson had the small oil-painted portrait of Eva Kingsley—painted two years ago, when she was seventeen—in his head; he would know her when he saw her, if she was not much changed.

Forward...

He was drowsing a bit, letting Phoenix lead the way. He could smell the damp of morning in the sultry air.

Forward, Nineteenth Alabama...!

And just that fast, it was upon him.

It had been a confused meeting of weary soldiers, on that early evening of April 6th, 1862, with the sun sinking down over the bloody forest and fields of Shiloh and the red-tinged Owl Creek swamp. "Forward, Nineteenth Alabama!" had been the cry sent up by a young Confederate captain who'd been a lawyer not so long before, but who had enlisted to do his duty for the Southland, been trained and stationed at Mobile for three months. He and his men had first seen the "elephant" this morning, as the grays attacked the blues to push them back into the swamp's embrace. The day's fighting had been long and brutal. Captain Lawson had already received the graze of a rifle ball across the meat of his right shoulder and a hole in his hat. The balls sounded like hornets as they passed, a deadly hum and whine that ended with the cries of many young men falling to their knees with their brains spilling out or the blood pooling where they lay. Waves of gunsmoke floated through the trees. In some places soldiers were nearly face-to-face in the deepening gloom before they recognized the colors of the enemy and pulled their triggers or swung their swords. Forward went the men of the Nineteenth Alabama, and forward to meet them in the darkening thickets came the men in Union blue.

Shots erupted along the ragged line. Fire and sparks flew into the tormented air. Lawson squeezed off a shot from his Navy Colt and was answered by a rifle slug that nearly kissed the right side of his face. Cannonfire boomed in the distance, cavalry horses shrieked and fell, and with his next step Lawson found himself boot-deep in a young soldier's entrails as the Union soldier sat on his knees and tried dazedly to push the red coils back in where they belonged.

"On the left! Riders on the left!" someone shouted. Lawson saw the enemy cavalry coming from that direction between the trees, sabers carving the air. He got off a shot and saw a man in an officer's uniform grasp at his throat and topple. The rebel soldier three feet to Lawson's left lost the top of his head to a gleaming saber, and Lawson fired into the rider's face but the horse was quickly past him and gone.

"Forward! Forward!" Lawson shouted, but what they were going forward to he did not know. Those were the orders. *Forward, ever forward, and not a step back until the Yanks are neck-deep in the Owl Creek swamp.* This day and now into the dusk he had seen carnage beyond his imagining. He had thrown up his guts, but at least they were still in his body.

Over the riflefire and shouting and the sound of horses and men being killed he heard the cannons speak in their deadly tongues of flame, and suddenly the blasts began on all sides. Plumes of dirt and broken rocks shot into the air. "Forward!" Lawson hollered, but he knew no one could hear. He staggered onward, with maybe a dozen of his men around him, and with a few paces taken they broke through the burning underbrush and into a hail of Union lead.

Soldiers fell to Lawson's left and right. One man grabbed at his arm as he went down, shot through the lung and bubbling blood. Lawson fired into the haze of smoke, the Colt kicking in his grip. A fierce pain stabbed his right thigh above the knee and stole his breath. A second slug hit him squarely in the left shoulder and knocked him back. He fell into the thicket of vines and thorns, and there he lay as the battle raged around him, his lungs hitching and his vision fading in and out. He told himself to get up, to rejoin the fight, and as he tried a body fell across him and pinned him down. Horses without riders thundered past. The cannons spoke again from a distance, and once more the earth exploded.

In this maelstrom of death and destruction Trevor Lawson sank down into what felt like a hole lined with velvet black. His eyes closed, and his body shivered as he slept.

He awakened in the dark, with the sounds of pain around him. He smelled blood and sulphur. The murmurs of wounded and dying men rose up from the forest like whispered hymns. Occasionally someone cried out or sobbed. Lawson could no longer hear the noises of battle. The cannons were silent. Frogs croaked from bloodied ponds and crickets chirped in the gore-smeared weeds. Lawson felt the throbbing pain of his bullet wounds. He thought his left shoulder might be broken, for he couldn't move that arm. He was aware that he yet gripped hard to the Colt. Was it still loaded? He didn't know. The body that lay across him twitched. Lawson could smell whiskey on the man's mouth. Confederate or Yank, he knew not, but the man was still breathing. Also the wounded soldier had a beard like the pride of a hog's bristle-brush. Lawson needed to push the man off, to roll him over, anything to get free. With one working arm it was going to be difficult. The man muttered something that sounded like *Lemons, Rolly* in his delirium, and Lawson wanted to say *Get off me, you damned fool.*

He was aware, then, that there was movement among the fallen soldiers.

There was no light. No candle-lit lanterns searching for those who might survive the night, to be loaded onto wagons and taken to the field hospital. There was no light, but there was movement.

Lawson turned his head to the left as much as he could. He could barely breathe with this bearded ox lying across him. He narrowed his eyes, scanning the dark. Yes...someone was moving among the bodies. More than one, it appeared. The figures were nearly blurred, moving like ghosts yet they were not spirits of the dead, for Lawson saw them crouch down and they became solid enough in their stillness. He counted five, and possibly there were more he could not see. He thought they might be camp followers looking for their lovers, for indeed three were women in long and dirtied gowns. He started to call out for help, to proclaim *I am alive*, but before he could summon the breath to speak...

...someone reached down and wrenched the bearded ox's head backward. Lawson saw long clawlike fingernails caked with dirt. The bearded man's throat was exposed; his eyelids fluttered, as if he were awakening from his wounded slumber. Then suddenly there were two figures crouching down on either side, a man and a woman both thin and wild-haired. The man wore a mud-stained dark suit, the woman a dirty light-colored gown with what appeared to be fabric roses at the bosom.

Lawson saw the woman open her mouth wide, and wider still. Something unhinged in the jaw and the lower teeth thrust forward. Two curved fangs descended from the upper teeth, and in a blurred rush of desperation of need or hunger she bit into the bearded man's throat on one side while the man's descended fangs plunged into the other side. Their eyes burned red at the centers, as if embers glowed there from the hearth of Hell.

Their bodies shuddered. The bearded man's eyes opened and rolled backward in his head to show the whites. His face contorted in silent agony. The two creatures continued to feed from his throat, making slurping and sucking noises. Tendrils of blood ran. The male creature's hand drifted out and stroked the woman's tangled hair, as if this moment was the essence of the greatest love between them.

Lawson made a noise. Maybe it was a gasp of shock or a whine of horror, he didn't know. But in the next instant the red-centered eyes of the two things were upon him, and as they pulled away from the offered throat blood drooled from their fangs. They sat on their haunches, observing him as one might observe a nice piece of juicy steak, the next object of their banquet.

With the cold sweat of fear on his face Lawson lifted his right arm, cocked the Colt and fired a bullet into the male creature's forehead.

The noise was deafening and caused some of the other creatures to shriek, an unholy sound of keening banshees. The thing that had just been shot sat staring at Lawson, his red eyes unblinking, his forehead slightly caved in and a hole smoking where the bullet had passed. Then he grinned, as if this were just the best of entertainments.

At the edge of madness Lawson shot the woman in the face. Her nose splintered into pieces like a china cup breaking and her head rocked back with a force that might have snapped a human's neck, but then she righted herself and her hand with its broken and filthy nails came up to touch the ragged hole. An expression of dismay flickered across the noseless and bloody-lipped visage, and she said to her companion in a voice like the whisper of dry wind through dead reeds: "Oh, Ezekiel, he has made me *ugly*."

Lawson shoved his right shoulder against the body that lay across him. He squirmed out from under the weight, as the wound at his thigh sought to drag him again down into a dark pool of pain. He was having none of it. Though gunshot in two places, Trevor Lawson realized that if he stayed in this place he would be consumed by these demons, and whether this was real or a fiction of his fevered brain made no matter. He wanted to, and intended to, live. Once free of the man's weight Lawson scrabbled like a broken crab across the ground, across bodies living and dead and pieces of bodies. He heard the high, ringing laughter of the things behind him, and he dared not look. With an effort that made the breath of agony whoosh from his lungs and fresh sweat jump from his pores he got up on his feet and, crashing through the bullet-riddled underbrush, he fled for his life.

They were after him fast enough, because he could hear their laughter all around him. One of them nipped at his left ear, like an evil kiss. A woman in a grimy green dress danced before him, making him change direction. A man in a formal suit, a tophat and a black waistcoat used a cane with a dog's head on it to strike lightly and mockingly at his face. Something that was missing its legs—a nightmare figure in the tatters of a Confederate uniform—came at him from the underbrush on its hands and stubs, its eyes glinting red and its fangs snapping at the air. A hand stroked the back of his head, almost in pity. A tongue licked his cheek, and Lawson smelled blood on the thing's mouth.

In that instant he almost lost his mind.

They were all around him, converging on the hobbling cripple who thought he might awaken in Alabama on a summer morning with the sun already hot in the trees and none of this—*none of this*—would have ever happened. He would go to the breakfast table in the house in Montgomery and meet his two angels, Mary Alice and Cassie, and there would be no more war or thoughts of war and no more horror upon horror.

Yet here, in this woods of Shiloh in the dark of a starless night, Trevor Lawson toppled over a fallen tree and went to the ground like a hunted beast. He crawled as best he could, and feeling them about to fall upon him he twisted around and fired the Colt and fired again but this time the hammer clicked on an empty chamber and all was lost.

Whether it was men or women or both who flung themselves upon him, he did not know. Whatever they were, they were strong and they were hungry. They were going for his throat, but he was being bitten on shoulders and chest, through his uniform and into the flesh.

They were licking the blood of his wounds with their tongues and forcing the wounds wider with their fangs. They were on him like worms on an apple, like ants on a piece of sugar candy; they swarmed him. He fought back, striking left and right with his Colt, for the revolver had become simply a blunt instrument. But though he fought and kept fighting he knew in his soul he was doomed because his blood was running and the fangs were sinking into his throat on both sides.

Abruptly one figure was thrown aside and then another. There was a mewling sound from bloodied mouths. The mass of creatures moved back, shoulders hunched like whipped dogs.

"*I* want this one," said the woman in red.

It had been nearly a whisper, but even so it carried force. She stood over Lawson, staring down upon him. A sweep of her hand pushed back her waves of black hair, and Lawson saw the beautiful high-cheekboned face of a fallen angel. She was regal in her evil; she wore it as grandly as she wore her earth-stained crimson gown. She smiled at him, a smile of triumph and need…and then in a blur of red she was at his throat.

He tried to push her away, tried to club at her with the Colt, but it was useless. He was weak and depleted; everything was becoming hazy and dreamlike. He felt the flow of his blood going into her, and he shuddered. He was growing cold. Still she drank of him. His mind was sluggish, but he realized he was being carried away by the blue canoe of death on its lazy current and he could no longer fight back. It was a matter of time now...a matter of time...

And then she drew back just short of taking him all, and he heard her as if from a great distance saying *This one goes with us* and he was picked up and carried through brush and thorns and scraped by treebark. Until he lost his senses and sank down again into the dark, and that was how it had begun.

Forward, Lawson thought as he rode Phoenix toward St. Benadicta and lit a cheroot. *Always forward.* His match flared in the dark. He was aware that his breathing was changing. It was becoming shallower, tighter, as if his lungs were becoming ever smaller. He wondered if his organs would in time shrivel and die, until he was a true creature of the Dark Society, and then he would have no more need of breathing the air of the human world.

That would happen if he became reliant solely on human blood. But the truth was, the desire for human blood was growing stronger and stronger in him, and unless he found LaRouge and killed her soon...and consumed from her the black ichor that ran through her veins as the blood of the vampire...he was doomed to eternal life as a monster of the night.

Right now, though, he was a gunslinger and adventurer who handled all matters for a price, and right now he had enough lungs left to enjoy one of his favored Marsh-Wheeling cheroots. He was alive and still mostly human. Mostly. He had a job to do, and that was enough for right now.

Five.

LAWSON FELT THE SUN SINKING. Always it was so, and never could he explain to Father Deale what that sensation was. Even wrapped like a mummy in his black curtains and hidden under bedsheets or sometimes under the bed or in a closet, he felt the sun sinking. With his eyes closed and his body in its state of sleep, he sensed the change of light in the hours, and then in the evening when the sun had almost gone he quickly came fully and often hungrily awake.

So it was, on this first night in St. Benadicta. The man in the black Stetson and the black suit with the white shirt, the crimson waistcoat and the gunbelt that holstered two backward-facing Colt pistols could never have been taken to be what he really was. When he walked down the stairs of the boarding-house and onto the dirt street—the only street—of St. Benadicta, the sun was nearly a memory and stars had begun to sparkle in the sky. No one would have thought that indeed he had secured a room early this morning and had slept not in its rather moldy bed but in its much more moldy closet, away from the broken shutters that allowed in a little too severe a sun for the gentleman's comfort.

His first drink of the evening had been cattle blood from a small Japanese bottle similar to the one that had broken in his coat the night before. He'd bought six of the things, all from the same Royal Street antiques dealer. It pleased him to be in possession of things of beauty, especially if they were functional.

He walked in the direction of the saloon, which was a flimsy wooden structure near the docks. The town, as much as it was, ended at the edge of the swamp. Logging boats and barges were tied up for the night. He would need a rowboat himself, for later. At the moment he needed information, as the gnarled old woman who ran the boarding-house had only told Lawson in her thick Cajun accent that Nocturne was "no mo'".

Fiddle music came from the direction of the Swamp Root, the name painted on the bar over the batwing doors. Yellow lantern light spilled out. Loggers staggered around, supported by flouncy women. Across the way was another building with Pleasure Palace painted in red on its front. It seemed to Lawson that St. Benadicta held only two activities for these lumberjacks when they weren't sawing timber in the morass out there. He avoided a collision between himself and a drunken bulk of a man who was being helped across the street by an equally drunk and bulky woman, and then he pushed through the doors into the Swamp Root.

The place was crowded, smoky and noisy and altogether disagreeable, but it was the only bar in town. Above Lawson, a couple of dozen old axeheads had been driven into the timbers and left there to grow red skins of rust. A bartender was busy pouring hard liquor and beer for thirsty and very loud patrons. The fiddler was doing his best, but every third note seemed to be a cat's squall. No one minded. Women wearing patchwork gowns and with feathers in their hair hung on the arms of florid-faced men who were spending their pay unwisely and too well. Lanterns hung from ceiling hooks and the candlelight jumped off broken teeth and the glint of coins. Lawson took a long look around. There were no vampires in here, only humans in need. He stepped up to the bar, caught the bartender's attention and asked for a small shot of whiskey, best in the house.

It came in a glass that was sufficiently clean. "We don't want no trouble, sir," said the bartender, as he set the whiskey down. His voice was nervous and he had a cocked left eye.

"No trouble," Lawson answered, with an attempt at a reassuring smile. He was aware that he looked the part of trouble, and that his pallid and rawboned appearance spoke of graves and death. When the Colts were in full view, so much the more. He was confident of his speed and his aim, and confident that no man would take him on without paying a price, and those confidences also spoke in his silence.

"A question for you," Lawson said as he put upon the bar the coin for his drink. "I'm looking for a town called Nocturne, south of here. Heard of it?"

"No sir. Ain't been here very long."

"Thank you anyway." Lawson looked at the heavy-set man on his right. "A town called Nocturne. Heard of it?"

"Don't know nothin' 'bout that," was the rather addled reply, for a nearly empty bottle of rotgut stood at his pleasure.

"A town called Nocturne?" Lawson asked the gray-bearded and wiry man on his left. "South of here? Do you know it?"

"Ain't nothin' south a'here," the man answered in a voice that might have put to shame the grind of a heavy bandsaw cutting through the hardest cypress. "Swamp and more swamp, is all." He took a swig from his mug of cloudy brown beer. "You got the city smell on ya. New Aw'luns?"

"That's right." Lawson mused on how many smells he could perceive in the Swamp Root, and how few of them were pleasant. The blood smell in here was nearly overpowering, that and cheap cigars, sweat, the smell of unwashed bodies and clothes, the tang of the sour beer and the sharp whiskey, and the occasional fragrance of feminine essence as one of the women brushed past.

"What're you doin' here, then?" The man took stock of Lawson's clothes and, being an intelligent fellow, came to a conclusion. "You ain't no lumberjack."

"No, I'm not."

"Oh, I got it! You're one of *them*! Am I right?"

Lawson maintained a slight smile. "One of *them*, sir?"

"You got a brother back there." The man motioned with a scarred thumb toward the rear of the Swamp Root. At a round table under the glow of lanterns sat a group of six gamblers playing cards. They were being watched by an interested audience of both loggers and whores. The 'brother' this man referred to was a broad-shouldered gent in a tan-colored suit and a Stetson the same hue, cocked at a jaunty angle. In front of him on the table was an impressive amount of currency and coins. The other players were all raggedy lumberjacks who had obviously been enticed to join this game by...

"A cardsharp," said the man. "Comin' in here on payday

and takin' candy from the babies. Ain't no use tellin' 'em, they ain't gonna listen."

"Hm," said Lawson, watching the cardsharp gently lay down what appeared to be a winning hand, for the others groaned and slapped their cards aside. Two of the loggers had had enough and left the table, but their places were quickly taken and the game continued. "Is he fleecing the sheep?" Lawson asked.

"Not so you'd know it. He loses enough to gull 'em. Never gets down so far he can't climb back up, though. Little babies, thinkin' they're gonna leave that table with some money for Mona. Heh! But listen here, ain't *you* one of his breed?"

"No, not his breed." Lawson was already picking up his shotglass and moving away. "But I don't like cheaters, so I think I'll go watch the game."

"Not sayin' he is for sure. That kinda thing'll get you killed, and he *is* wearin' a six. But get in there and gull *him*, if you can. You look like you're able."

Lawson made his way back. If anything, he might find someone who knew Nocturne. As he neared the table, he saw the cardsharp glance up quickly from the cards at his approach and then back to business again. But in that brief instant Lawson had seen a broad apple-cheeked face with a cleft in the chin, thick reddish eyebrows and below them deep-set dark eyes. The man had a friendly, easy and relaxed composure, but also in that brief instant Lawson had seen a black glimmer of warning in the eyes and a tightening of the beefy shoulders, the message being *approach me with caution.*

That was like a summons to Trevor Lawson, who sipped at his whiskey and brought up his predator's smile.

He took a position alongside the table, where he could watch everyone. They were playing Five Card Draw with deuces wild. The cardsharp raised the pot to two hundred dollars and then folded. On the next hand, he was the first to fold. Lawson watched the man lose forty dollars on the following hand to a pair of tens and a deuce. The cardsharp removed his hat, mopped his brow with a handkerchief and then returned the hat, and that was when Lawson saw how he kept the cards up his sleeve. The man was very quick and very smooth, but he was not quicker and smoother than the vampire's eye. The next hand he won sixty dollars by way of two jacks and two deuces.

One of the other loggers decided retreat was the better course of valor and left the table. "Join in?" Lawson asked, and everyone but the cardsharp nodded. Lawson said, "Thank you," and took a seat opposite the man.

"Five dollars to play, friend," the cardsharp said without meeting Lawson's gaze. Lawson put down his money, and the game continued.

The fiddler scratched on. The bartender poured beer and whiskey. Two men got in a fight and went crashing through the batwing doors into the dirt. The game went on, with Lawson up by twenty dollars and everyone but the cardsharp doing reasonably well. Biding his time, Lawson thought. And sizing me up as well.

In the yellow light, the floating cigar, cigarette and pipe smoke and the fetid mist that rose from the water and drifted into the saloon, Lawson was aware that someone else had entered the Swamp Root and had come back to watch the game. He smelled her before he saw her. She was maybe twenty-four or twenty-five years old. She brought with her the aromas of lavender, leather, lemon soap and hot blood. When he gazed into her eyes he saw two bits of hard black charcoal, aimed at him. Her full-lipped mouth looked like it could bite the head off a water moccasin. She was tall and lithe and had light brown hair tied back in a ponytail. On her head was a dark green jockey's cap. She wore a gray skirt and a black riding jacket over a white-and-green checked blouse. Her chin was firm and square and her nose was sharp and tilted up at the tip. Then Lawson took appreciative note of the intricately-tooled wheat-colored gunbelt slung on her slim waist, holding a couple of dozen bullets and a Remington revolver with a mother-of-pearl grip.

Lawson lost the following hand to a thin lumber-jack with maybe six teeth in his head and black hair that had been cut under a soupbowl. The cardsharp paused to have a sip of his own whiskey, and his eyes too found the young woman who'd just arrived. A few other men came forward to test the air, and finding it too rare for them they retreated, especially when the new arrival casually rested a black-gloved hand on the butt of her pistol.

"I'm Neville Brannigan," said the man across the table from Lawson. "From Houston, Texas." He offered a hand that was the perfect size to be slipping cards in and out of sleeves.

"Is there any other Houston?" Lawson asked, shaking the man's hand in a quick, firm and cold grip. He saw Brannigan's eyes narrow. "Trevor Lawson, from New Orleans." Lawson wondered if Brannigan had really been introducing himself to the young woman with the six-shooter.

"Might I ask what business you have in St. Benadicta?"

"Passing through." It was Lawson's turn to deal. He spent a moment squaring the deck. "Looking for another town, actually. Ever heard of a place called Nocturne?"

"No. And I will say, Mr. Lawson, that there is nowhere from here to pass through *to*. This is as far as civilization goes."

"Anyone else heard of Nocturne?" Lawson asked the others at the table, and got either the shaking of heads or blank stares. "Well, then," he said, "I suppose it's hidden." He offered the deck to the man on his left to cut. "But I'm sure I'll find it."

"What about this particular Nocturne is so appealing to you, sir?" Brannigan opened a silver cigarette case and removed a freshly-rolled stick. He used his thumb to fire the match.

"I have business there. In fact, I'm expected. Now... about yourself...you are a mainstay here? Or also passing through?"

"I am an *entertainment* here," was the smooth reply, accompanied by a cloud of smoke. "I make the circuit of the logging towns, to give these fine men something on which to focus their energies besides the obvious. In that way I do my part for the common good." He smiled, showing a gold tooth at the front of his mouth. The smile didn't last very long, and was replaced by a narrowed-eyed expression of curiosity. "You are very *pale*, sir. Why is that?"

"I have an unfortunate condition," said Lawson, as he prepared to deal. "Also...like you, Mr. Brannigan...I work at night. Same game?"

"Absolutely," said the cardsharp, tapping ashes upon the floorboards.

When the cards were dealt, Lawson had a queen of spades, a four of clubs, a six of clubs, an ace of diamonds and an ace of hearts. Brannigan instantly raised the ante to fifty dollars, which made two of the other players fold. Lawson saw the raise and raised another fifty. Brannigan saw the raise and studied his cards with

I TRAVEL BY NIGHT

a blank expression. The other two loggers at the table folded. Brannigan took one card, Lawson discarded his clubs cards and took two. He wound up with a queen of spades, an ace of diamonds, an ace of hearts, a ten of hearts and a seven of spades. Not very good, he thought... but good enough.

"Fifty dollars," said Brannigan.

"Fifty, and raise fifty," replied the vampire from New Orleans.

"*Really?*" Brannigan smiled across the table, but his eyes were cold. "Well...it's getting a little hot in here, gents." He laid his cards down face-up, took his handkerchief from his breast pocket and started to take his hat off to wipe his forehead.

"Mr. Brannigan?" said Lawson, in a voice that commanded the cardsharp's attention. When that happened, Lawson threw his Eye.

Lawson wasn't sure how he did this, only that when he wanted to—and the need was there—it was simply a matter of a little mental concentration. In fact, it was getting easier. He envisioned a flaming eyeball pushing itself out of his forehead, and travelling across the distance of a few feet to the forehead of another man, where it winnowed itself in and disappeared, still burning. And there in the man's brain it threw a light, as it moved through the corridors of memory. These corridors might have been the hallways of a haunted house, for Lawson had learned that all men carried their ghosts. Many of these spirits were sad, many were hideous to look upon. The flaming Eye moved within Neville Brannigan's head, and Brannigan wore a crooked smile and his own eyes had glazed over. The cardsharp's hand was still reaching for his hat. Lawson saw quick images of Texas prairie and ramshackle farmhouses surrounded by tumbleweeds and blowing dust. He thought this was more Lubbock than Houston, and maybe Brannigan had reason to lie about his hometown. He saw a farmhouse on fire and a woman holding a child to her breast as she fled through the dust. He saw a shadowy figure advancing across a room that had a picture of Jesus hanging on the wall, and in the shadowy figure's hand was a knife. He saw a man on his knees, bleeding from the mouth and nose, and a knife going into the back of the man's neck. He saw a black horse rearing up, and a whip swinging out, and he heard a woman's scream that chilled the dying marrow of his bones. He saw cards by the hundreds, and faces around the tables, and he saw a young boy with curly blonde hair being beaten by the butt of a pistol in a small dank room where light itself seemed a stranger.

It was not Lawson's intent to interpret these ghosts. They just existed here, in this man's mind. By trial and error, Lawson had also learned that the Eye served the purpose of searing with its flames his victim's strength of will. With the Eye roaming free in a man's memory, that individual was reduced to a mass of flesh whose mind belonged to the vampire.

"Show us your hidden cards," said Lawson.

Brannigan was still smiling crookedly, his eyes beginning to twitch and water. He was yet strong, and he was trying to resist.

"Show us," Lawson repeated, "your hidden cards." His gaze was impassive, his voice slow and deliberate. "Show us *now*."

Brannigan trembled. His mouth opened as if to protest, and the gold tooth sparked light. But he did not speak, for his senses had abandoned him.

He reached into his left sleeve and brought out an ace of spades, which fell from his fingers onto the table. Reaching into his right sleeve brought a deuce of clubs fluttering down.

"I'll be damned!" growled one of the lumberjacks. "Lookit! Bastard's been cheatin' us!"

"*Silence*," Lawson said, a quiet but firm command that was best obeyed. "Mr. Brannigan, show us your hand."

It seemed the cardsharp wanted to twist his head to both sides, but his neck seemed too tight. His face was sweating. His fingers trembled as he turned his cards over. He revealed a five of clubs and a five of diamonds, a four of hearts, a jack of diamonds and a ten of clubs.

Lawson turned his cards over, and stared into Brannigan's watery eyes. He brought his own flaming Eye back from the haunted hallways, and said, "I think a pair of aces wins this pot, sir."

The flaming Eye left Brannigan's forehead and floated across the table back into Lawson's possession. The cardsharp had turned nearly as pale as the vampire. He shuddered and made a sick moaning noise, as if he were about to puke all over the table, the cards, the money and everything. Lawson raked the money toward himself before it could be vomited upon.

The lumberjacks were standing up, red-faced and angry. Brannigan was staring dumbly at his cards, and at the two cards that had been hidden. "What...*happened?*" he asked, a thread of saliva breaking over his lower lip. "My God...what happened...?"

"You skunked us, you bastard!"

"Sonofabitch, we don't suffer cheaters!"

Something seemed to click in the cardsharp's brain. Brannigan looked across the table at Lawson, and at the pile of money, and suddenly the man snarled like an animal and he was standing up, throwing his chair backward. His right hand went into his coat. Lawson saw the holster and the revolver there, and the man was fast but Lawson was supernaturally faster. He already had the Colt with the rosewood grip up in Brannigan's face before the cardsharp's six could clear leather.

"Let's not get too angry," Lawson said quietly. "Bad for the health."

Brannigan's hand left his pistol. Then he remained still, his fearful gaze fixed on the business end of Lawson's gun.

The fiddler had ceased his squalling. The place had hushed and all attention was focused on the little drama at the card table. One of the loggers who'd stood up shouted, "Damn him, he stole more'n a hundred dollars of my money! I say he swings!"

"Yeah, hang the bastard!" another one hollered.

"Now look what you've started," Lawson said to the hapless cardsharp. He also stood up, and noted that the young woman with the holstered six-shooter had moved back into the throng and was gone. "Hold on, all of you!" he told the crowd as they moved forward. "Maybe he can pay his way out of a lynching? Nasty way to leave this earth. Mr. Brannigan, if I were you I'd give up every cent of the money I won. Put it on the table. Then put your gun on the table, turn around and walk out of here, get your horse and *go*. The sooner the better."

"Hell, no!" shouted the first lumberjack who'd wanted a hanging. "He cheated us, he gets a damned necktie party!"

Brannigan was already emptying his pockets. Coins and bills were flung to the table, followed by the man's gun.

Lawson kept his Colt somewhere between Brannigan and the crowd. "You don't want to hang anybody tonight, gents," he said easily. "Your money's here. Collect it as you please. But killing this man because he was stupid and greedy? Get the law down here on you? No. I say let him walk."

"Well, then…break his legs, is what I say!" yelled a black-bearded behemoth who looked like he could do this deed with one hand.

"Let him *walk*," Lawson repeated, staring into the man's fierce blue eyes. He restrained throwing his own burning Eye until he had to. "Want him out of town *now*? Then step back and let him go. Take your money and be pleased to have it." He paused, waiting to deflect any-more threats, but none came. He hated cheaters, but he didn't care for a lynch mob either. "Mr. Brannigan, you see the way out. I'd go while you can."

The cardsharp cast Lawson a look that may have been either grudging thanks or a faceful of hatred, but he got himself moving. A few men blocked his way and caused him to either move around them or squeeze between. On the way past the bar someone threw their beer in his face, and someone else added a glistening yellow egg of spit to his cheek. Then Brannigan was out the batwing doors and gone, the fiddler started up again and the noise did too and Lawson put his gun away and gathered up his own money. He took a beer that was sent to him from the bar, sipped it and set it aside because it wasn't to his taste. He needed a little cattle blood to make it palatable. He spent awhile talking to some loggers about finding Nocturne and none of them knew the place. Where to rent a boat? he asked, and was told to look for McGuire at the dock.

Lawson left the Swamp Root and headed for the water. The darkness of the swamp beckoned him. He was walking past the stable when the image of a picture of Jesus hanging on a wall jumped into his mind. He smelled beer and caught a figure coming up from a shadow to his right, and as he whirled around with a speed no human could match the knife in Brannigan's hand went for his neck.

Six.

BY THE TIME LAWSON *THOUGHT* of what he should do, he was doing it. His arm came up in a blur and grasped the cardsharp's knifehand to stop the fall of the blade, and he prepared himself to throw the fool through the nearest window.

But before he could put that thought into action, a pistol shot cracked and the knifeblade broke in front of Lawson's face. A second shot, delivered on the powder-smoke of the first, lifted Brannigan's hat off his head and sent it spinning. Brannigan bleated with terror, all intent to do harm forgotten. He wrenched desperately to get free of his captor, who had ducked low to avoid any more flying lead. Then Lawson let Brannigan go and the man ran for his life, in the opposite direction of the swamp. Lawson aimed a kick at his tail, but the cardsharp's speed of terror beat the vampire's half-hearted vengeance and so Brannigan scurried away into the night whimpering like a little lost child.

From a crouched position, Lawson drew both pistols and surveyed the darkness. He saw the gray gunsmoke hanging in a narrow alleyway. Just that fast, the vampire gunslinger sped forward to the mouth of the alley, where he flattened himself against a wall of rough planks. Nothing moved beyond. He heard the noise of shouting. People were coming to find out what the shooting was about. Lawson eased into the alley, both revolvers ready, but his red-centered eyes detected no threat. *Damnation*, he thought. *Somebody shooting at me or at Brannigan?* Whoever had pulled the quick-fire trigger, they were gone.

And so too, he decided, he ought to be.

He slipped away and became one with the dark. He holstered his guns, but kept his eyes aimed. In another few minutes he rounded a roughhewn building and found himself at the dock where the logging boats were tied up. Beyond lay the absolute darkness of the swamp, but on the dock was a cabin that showed lamplight through the windows. Lawson knocked at the door and waited.

It opened with a billow of sour whiskey smell into Lawson's face. A wizened old man with a scraggly white beard and white eyebrows that jumped like angry snakes peered out, a blue jug of Rose's Whiskey gripped in his hand. He was bald, his head blotched with age spots burned in by the sun. A razor scar began at the left side of his mouth and progressed nearly to the ear. His nose had been broken more than twice. He wore a faded and ragged pair of overalls, his chest bare and showing a boil of white hair. He narrowed his dark little eyes. "Whazzit?" he asked, in a voice like the grating of stone against stone.

"McGuire?"

"I am. Who're *you*?"

"Trevor Lawson, from New Orleans. You're the dockmaster here?"

"*Dockmaster?*" McGuire gave a nasty chortle. "I watch the boats at night. Work on 'em some if they need work. Keep the records of who goes out and where they're goin'. That make me a dockmaster?"

"It does."

"Then," McGuire took a swig of his liquor, "I reckon I is." He offered a thin-lipped smile that lasted only a few seconds. "What're you wantin' with *me*?"

"I need a boat. A small skiff, something with two oars. Got anything that'll do?"

McGuire hesitated, as if thought he hadn't heard this right. "A *skiff*," he repeated. "You're from New Orleans and you come here to this damned shit-hole to take a skiff out into Hell's Acres? What's your business? Runnin' away from a nuthouse?"

"I'm sane," Lawson answered, though sometimes he doubted it. "I'm looking for a town called Nocturne."

McGuire laughed, but his eyes weren't in it. "Now I know you're an *in*-sane idjit! Ain't no town called Nocturne out there! And I know that swamp, as much as any man does. Much as any man *wants* to know it!"

"No town called Nocturne?" Lawson prodded. "You're sure of that?"

The dockmaster took another drink of what was most likely both his courage and his pride. "Sure there ain't one *now*. Nocturne was wiped out near sixteen years ago."

"Ah." A ray of light in this eternal midnight, he thought. "Wiped out how?"

"Hurricane. Came tearin' in from the Gulf and flooded the town. That was August of 1870."

Lawson nodded. "May I come inside for a few minutes?"

"No!" came the quick response. "This is my *home*! I don't suffer no idjits here."

A hand into a pocket and the production of a five-dollar gold piece made McGuire put down the jug he'd been lifting to his mouth.

"Come right on in," said the dockmaster, opening the door wider. He took the gold piece as Lawson entered, and then closed the door behind.

The place was a hermit's heaven. All the furniture—chairs, table, bed—looked to have been hammered together by a crooked man using a crooked hammer. There stood a cast-iron stove rimmed with rust. On the planked floor was a red rug that looked like a dog had been chewing on it, but there was no dog. The walls were bare boards and even the lamplight looked dirty.

"My castle," said McGuire, with just an edge of sarcasm. "Welcome to it."

Lawson had seen worse. He'd been trapped in worse. He decided not to sit. "Nocturne," he said. "Tell me where it is."

"Out there." McGuire hooked a gnarled thumb toward the swamp. "Off the main channel to the west, about five miles as the crow flies. What the hell you wantin' with Nocturne?" His eyes studied Lawson's clothes. "New Orleans gent. But somethin' ain't right with you, is it?"

"No," said Lawson.

"You smell funny. Cold, like a grave."

"My nature," was the answer, delivered calmly and quietly. "Everyone else I asked about Nocturne tonight didn't know it. Why do you?"

"I used to live there, bucko." McGuire sat down at the crooked table. He set the jug aside and placed the gold coin before him so he could admire it. "Got anymore of these?"

"Enough for a skiff with two oars."

"I reckon you do. Drink?" He tapped the jug with two knuckles.

"Not my brand. I want to leave for Nocturne within the hour."

"Now there's a story in *this*!" McGuire grinned wickedly across the lamplit room at the vampire. "Goin' to Nocturne at *night*? Goin' to a ghost town in the dark of the swamp? Holy Mary, you *did* get out a nuthouse window, didn't you?"

"I'm sane enough," said Lawson. *But barely so*, he thought. "You say Nocturne is a ghost town? Destroyed by a hurricane? What else?"

McGuire took a long drink and turned the gold coin between his fingers. "Not all destroyed. Some of the mansions are still there, but they're half-ate up by the swamp. See, Nocturne was built on higher ground. Well, it was higher ground *then*. Fella who built it was a strange sort. A young man from a rich family. Came into the loggin' business to compete with his father, they had a kinda rivalry goin' on. Young fella was a little out of his mind, is what all us jacks figured. Well...maybe a *lot* out of his mind. We heard his father was a bully, ragged that young fella all the time about bein' worthless. So he spent money, time and labor buildin' an opera house and concert hall out in the swamp. Buildin' big mansions for himself and his business partners, but they didn't stay very long when they saw what he was doin'. Tryin' to build another New Orleans, make a port out of it. Puttin' all his money in makin' a fancy town where the 'gators used to drop their eggs and the snakes coiled in the mud by the hundreds. Then that hurricane hit." McGuire angled the coin so lamplight touched it and laid the color of gold across his scarred face. "Oh, Almighty God...that was a blower," he said quietly. "A monster, that thing was. Flew in on black wings, it did, in the middle of the night. Brought the swamp and the creatures of the swamp right into those workmen's houses, into those company stores, into that church and school and the opera house and concert hall and right into those mansions. Everything that wasn't blowed away or flattened was flooded. The dock and all the equipment destroyed. It was like...a punishment from God, for pushin' too far. You know what I'm sayin'?" He looked to the vampire for understanding.

"I do," said Lawson.

"I thought you would. You've got the look on you."

"And what might that be?"

"The look of somebody who knows what it's like to be punished by God," said McGuire. "I have been too. Lost my wife and a fine son in that storm. At dusk one day I was fifty, and at daybreak the next I was eighty. But time heals every hurt, they say. You believe that?"

Lawson was silent, because he didn't know what he believed.

"Yeah," said McGuire, who reached again for the jug of Roses, "I'm still waitin' too." When he finished drinking, he ran a hand over his face and sat staring at the wall for a moment as if he'd forgotten he had company in his castle. Then he said, "Twenty dollars, I'll give you a skiff with two oars. You won't make Nocturne tonight, though. Tomorrow sometime. That's best, you don't want to try to get there in the dark, you'll never find it. I'll get you a boat with a torch holder, fix you up. That'll help. When you wantin' to leave?"

"An hour at the most. I have to get some things from my room."

McGuire cocked his head to one side, as if to get a better view of his visitor. "All right, what's your business ought to stay your business...but I'm damned if I can figure out what *this* is about."

"I need to go to Nocturne." Lawson was already reaching for the gold coins. "That's all you have to know. I'll return the boat when I can. I'd also like you to draw me a map of how to get there. I'll pay extra for that. Oh... one other thing: the name of the young man who founded Nocturne. Would that name be Christian Melchoir?"

"That's right," said McGuire. "How'd you know?"

"I suspected. It seems Mr. Melchoir has an affinity for the place he created. He wants to give it..shall we say...a new life." Lawson walked forward and placed the coins on the table. "One hour," he said. "I thank you for your help."

"Thank me when you get back."

Lawson left that statement unanswered. He departed McGuire's cabin and, walking warily with an eye to the shadows and his hands ready to draw his Colts, he returned to the boarding-house. It didn't take him very long to get ready. He had what he needed, and what Father Deale had secured for him. Everything was in the saddlebags and he had two folded-up black window curtains. He would need these, if he was caught by the daylight out there. The thought didn't disturb him too much; if he was contained by the sunlight, so would they also be. He left the boarding-house and returned to McGuire's cabin, where the old logger who knew the punishment of God was waiting for him out front with a flaming torch. They walked together along the dock to where a few battered skiffs were tied up amid the larger workboats and barges, and McGuire pointed out the boat Lawson was to take. At its stern was a wooden socket where the torch could be placed. McGuire slid the torch in and put two oars in the oarlocks.

He climbed back up on the dock. He looked out into the darkness. Behind them and at a distance, the fiddler was still playing at the Swamp Root. Lawson heard the laughter of men and women who lived in another world.

"You sure you want to do this?" McGuire asked.

"I'm sure I *have* to do it." Lawson turned and scanned the vista of the dirty little town at his back. He was being watched; he was certain of it. Maybe one of the Dark Society was here, checking his progress. He stepped into the boat and put down his saddlebags and the folded black curtains. He didn't bother to remove either his coat or his Stetson, because even though the night was sultry and the swamp steamed, he no longer broke a sweat. He settled himself on the plank seat and took up the oars.

"Good luck," said McGuire as he untied the skiff's rope that bound it to the dock.

"Thank you, sir," Lawson answered, and then he began to row between the larger workboats toward the great dark expanse of the swamp. The torch burned at his back, but whether the light was welcome or not was an open question. He kept rowing slowly and steadily, as the town fell away behind. The fiddler's music and the sound of civilization faded away. The humming, chirring noise of the swamp—a true nocturne—rose to meet him.

He had a map drawn by McGuire in his coat pocket. He'd already looked it over, but there was time for further study later. In another few minutes the channel curved to the right and the last lights of St. Benadicta were hidden by the tangle of underbrush and moss-draped cypress trees. Lawson paused to let the boat drift and to light up a cigar using the torch. He exhaled smoke with his dwindling breath. He noted swarms of mosquitoes, but none would bite him; he wasn't warm enough for their tastes, and he figured that for the biting insects here he already exuded a smell of the dead.

His time, he realized full well, was running out.

He continued rowing, as the swamp enveloped him.

Something keened from a tree to his left. The darkness pulsed. Lawson smoked his cheroot and stared forward.

Shapes seemed to emerge from the night. They were the phantoms of what had been. He saw his boyhood home in Alabama and a favored dog that used to run with him. He saw a lake near his house where the fishing was always good. He saw a patch of forest and a cemetery where his ancestors lay, and who might have ever thought that he had a chance at eternal life if he only gave up his humanity and joined completely and totally with the Dark Society?

It was the stuff of nightmares, this death in life.

He had twice gone to visit his wife and daughter, after the events at Shiloh. He had twice gone to the house in Montgomery, in the concealing night, to press himself against a window and wish himself back with his loved ones. The first time, in a driving thunderstorm, the flash of a bolt of lightning had revealed him, and Cassie must have awakened and seen him through the glass, for her scream had sent him running. The second time, years later, he had followed Mary Alice on an evening in May, and noted that she had aged and was walking more slowly, and under the paper lanterns at a festival in the park she met the young woman Cassie had turned into. Also at that park was a handsome young man who held Cassie's hand, and Lawson's daughter held the hand of a little blonde-haired girl in a pink frock, and perhaps this was among the most cruel moments because everyone was so happy and the brass band's music was bright and the world had kept turning while Lawson fought the demons.

He had not stayed long at the festival. He had not let himself get very close to Mary Alice, or Cassie, or the young man his little girl had married and the child who was his grand-daughter. He had stayed far apart, in the darkness, and he had shivered because he smelled so much warm blood and he was so in need. And at last he had fled that scene of happiness and torture, and thought that somewhere in the family cemetery his gravestone was probably there but his grave was empty, for he was one of the more than three thousand missing or captured soldiers at Shiloh who had never come home.

That night he had almost drained to death a vagrant at the trainyards, but he had stopped short of killing the man. After that, he had to find out how strong he was, and how much he could endure, for he was not a monster and did not intend to become one.

Lawson kept rowing, and as the dark water chuckled around him and the insects flew about him but did not bite for his ichor was a bitter wine, he knew he was on his way to an evil destination where evil creatures sought to destroy him with a young girl's life in the balance.

But he travelled by night. It said so on his business card, along with *All Matters Handled*. He had been a lawyer, a husband and father, a soldier, and now…a vampire fighting to hold onto what remained of his humanity, and by doing so putting himself in harm's way for many humans who needed his help, for he was truly an 'adventurer' now, to keep his wits and his mind sharp and what remained of his human heart beating.

He would not give up the rest of himself to Christian Melchoir or any denizen of the Dark Society without a battle that would fracture the world. When he passed away from this earth, he desired to die as a human, and there was only one way.

Grim and determined, Lawson travelled on toward morning.

Seven.

HE HEARD THE BOAT COMING long before it reached him. He heard the slide of the oars and the movement of the green water. He waited, wrapped up in his black shrouds in the shadows of the cypress trees, as the boat neared. In another moment he smelled above the foulness of the swamp the aromas of lavender, leather, lemon soap and hot blood. He knew then who had been watching him last night, and now following him. He waited, one hand on the Colt with the rosewood grip, for her to bring her skiff nearly alongside. Then all was silent except for the gurgle of gas bubbles rising from the bottom and the croaking of hundreds of frogs in their slimy soup. He knew she was sitting there looking at him, trying to make heads-or-tails of this. He tensed only a little bit, when he heard her slide her six from her holster and cock it, but she noted the movement.

"Come out of there," she commanded.

He yawned under his veil.

"Did you hear me? Come out!"

"It'll take me a minute or two," Lawson answered. "You won't let that shooter go off, will you?"

"Just do what I say."

"Yes, ma'am. Forgive me if I'm a little cranky. This is not my best time of the—"

She fired a shot into the air that made birds shriek in the trees and for a few seconds silenced the frogs.

"Day," Lawson finished. He released the Colt's grip, winnowed his hands out and began to unwrap himself. Though he was covered by deep shadow, the glare of sun off the water was painful to him. It was, at best, a needles-and-pins sensation that grew more painful by the minute and at worst was the sensation that his flesh was being burned off his bones. He moved slowly and carefully to free himself, as his joints were sore. His temples throbbed and his teeth ached. When his head—minus his Stetson—emerged from the shroud, he saw the young woman draw back through the dark-tinted goggles that gave a measure of protection to his eyes. Even with the dark lenses, he had to narrow his eyes against the glare; they felt dried-out and tormented by small pieces of grit.

Lawson got his shoulders and the rest of his arms free. He sat up in his boat, which was roped to the nearest cypress. The pistol in the girl's hand was aimed at his chest. She had on the same clothes and dark green jockey's cap she'd been wearing in the Swamp Root, except now they were wet with sweat. The eyes in her otherwise attractive face were the same hard bits of coal. She was wearing her pair of black leather gloves to guard her hands against the rough wood of the oars. She was the type of woman, he mused, who came prepared. "Well," Lawson said, his vision filmy in the glare. He worked up a smile from the tight muscles of his pallid face. "Here we are."

"Yes," she replied.

"That's all? You're not going to ask me why I'm wrapped up like this and sleeping in my boat at...what time is it? Ten o'clock?"

"Near enough."

"I'll ask *you* some questions, then. You fired a shot that broke the gambler's knife, yes? And then shot the hat off his head? Very good shooting. You must be an expert. But why do that? Because you thought he was going to kill me? And you wanted me alive? Slow me down if I'm going too fast."

"You're on the tracks," she said.

"Your name is...?"

"Annie Remington."

"Hm," said Lawson. "That's a Remington Army pistol in your hand. I'm suspecting that's a professional name. You're a trick shooter? Travel for the company?"

"Maybe."

"Your *real* name is…?"

She paused for a moment, but Lawson already knew what she was going to say. "Ann Kingsley."

He nodded. "Eva's older sister. I saw her portrait. You do resemble each other. Your father told you everything? So you came here to make sure of exactly *what*?"

"I came here," said Ann Kingsley, staring directly into the orbs of Lawson's goggles, "to find out what kind of game you're playing with my sister's life." The Remington pistol never wavered. "How you got my father—a sensible man—to agree to this, I have no idea. But I'm not letting you out of my sight. And I sure as hell didn't want that gambler killing you last night before I had a chance to kill you…if I have to."

"I see," said the vampire. He scratched his smooth chin. "You think I had something to do with Eva's kidnapping?"

"I don't know what I think. I just know I'm burrin' to your saddle."

"That's a complication I'd rather not have."

"Do tell."

Lawson considered his position. The gunshot would hurt and might break a bone or two, but he'd survive it. He could rush her and take the gun, if this sunlight wasn't sapping his strength and speed. He could send his Eye into her head and command her to hand the pistol over, but he thought she might put up some strong resistance. He would win, in the end, but still…

Maybe she ought to keep her little piece of power, he decided. Could be useful, before all was said and done.

But still…

"You have no idea what you're dealing with," he said, which sounded like the most hackneyed statement ever made but was in this case horrifically true. "You don't want to stay around me, Miss Kingsley. And you surely do not want to go to Nocturne."

"Do tell again," she replied, with a derisive curl of her upper lip.

"Mercy me," Lawson said. "I suppose you won't take it on faith that I had nothing to do with all this, and that I intend to pay the ransom and return your sister unharmed?" Relatively speaking, he thought. What she'd witnessed might have already driven her mad. Or…she might have already been turned.

"I don't have that much faith. Or stupidity. Explain to me why you of all people were asked to take that ransom money in. *Why?*"

"Lucky," said Lawson.

"Don't think that's just it. Think there's a whole lot more you're not telling."

Lawson reached for his hat and put it on, because even in the shadow the sun was scorching his head. His skin was prickling, getting painful. "I'm going to wrap myself up again and go back to sleep. If you'll leave me alone, I'll wake up around sundown. Then we'll talk some more. Agreed?"

"No." Her gaze studied the black curtains. "Why aren't you sweating?" she asked. "And why are you... sleeping in the daytime, wrapped up in those?"

"A long story," was the answer.

"I have time. So do you."

"No, I really don't." He managed a grim smile. "You see, I'm in pain right now. It's still manageable...but I've got to get covered up. My skin. It's not suited to the sun. The longer I stay exposed—even in this shade—the worse the pain becomes." He paused to let that sink in. "Will you show me a little understanding?"

"I don't understand any of this," Ann said. But then some of the hardness left her eyes and she lowered the six. "You're very...strange," she offered.

"Strange. Tired. And hurting." He removed the Stetson and began to fold himself back into the black wings. "Please don't take it on yourself to go any further from here. You need me more than you know." It had occurred to him that though the citizens of Nocturne were also nightwalkers and were surely in their own cocoons and hiding places until sundown, there might be snares in the swamp left ready to trap the unwary daytime visitor, be it a curious logger or a politician's daughter. He would hate for someone as pretty as Ann Kingsley to wind up with a faceful of metal spikes. "Swear it," he added.

"I'm not swearing anything." Even though she'd said it with force, she immediately softened her tone. "I said I'm not letting you out of my sight. I meant it."

"That's good." Lawson had almost submerged himself into the shroud again, except for his goggled face. "I hope you enjoy fighting off mosquitoes until sundown. If I were you, I'd go back the way you came and leave this to me."

"I'll stay," she said, "and fight."

"No doubt you will. You might want to get some sleep, if you can. It may be a long night." So saying, he folded the curtains over his face and left Ann Kingsley to her own designs.

He slept in the way of vampires, one part deeply tranced and gathering strength for the night, another part on edge, senses questing, fearful of the pain of sunlight like a darktime insect. He'd had much time to think, and considered that this pain was as much mental as it was physical; it was the pain of a body losing its fluids and withering up toward the death in life, yes, but it was also the pain of separation from light and life, and the more religious the person had been the more the shame and agony of what he or she had become.

Lawson shifted in his edgy trance, his senses telling him that time was moving and the sun also but that Ann Kingsley was still there, dozing in her skiff and swatting with a gloved hand at the bugs that bit her face. In the haunted halls of his own memory he saw the little ruined town where the creatures had taken him that night after the battle at Shiloh. He saw the farmhouse where they took him down into a root cellar and roped his wrists and ankles to an iron bedframe and a thin, gore-stained mattress, and standing back they allowed the evil angel in red to approach with a single candle that illuminated her vulpine face. Sitting beside him on the mattress, she had traced with a fingernail his jawline and the slope of his nose, and she had leaned forward and whispered in his ear in her French-accented voice of dead reeds and dust, *"I am called LaRouge, and I have lived for a very long time. Do you know how long?"*

Of course he couldn't answer. He had been nearly bled dry already. He made a noise like the bleat of a sheep, but no sense.

"One hundred and forty-one years," she'd said, defying the fact that she appeared to be no more than twenty. Her bruise-colored tongue had emerged from her mouth, shivered like the tail of a rattlesnake and scraped like sandpaper along his cheek. When she was done with that, she smiled at him with her blood-crusted lips and her eyes shone green in the solitary light. "I have enjoyed many," she'd confided, whispering yet. "I have turned many, from what they were to what I wished them to be. Oh, some gave themselves to me willingly, for the gift I could return to them. Some fought, as you did. But you see…it's a losing battle. What is your name, soldier?"

He couldn't speak his name, and wouldn't even if he had had the power of speech.

It was then he felt her Eye enter his head and roam the mansion he had built of his life, and he writhed because she was everywhere, all the scenes of his life had her in them somewhere, as if she had been there all along but an invisible presence even at his own birth, when he walked the roads of his childhood, at his wedding, at the birth of his daughter, when he worked in his office scribing legal documents on a dark blue blotter, when he had gone to the Court House and volunteered to fight for the South. She was there when he wrote his name on the crisp piece of yellow paper.

"Trevor Lawson," whispered LaRouge, her crusted lips up close to his ear. "You're a very handsome man. You've had a fine life, haven't you? A very *noble* life. Well, Trevor…I'm going to make you my finest creation."

Such was the beginning of his fall from humanity, as much as into a bottomless pit.

Darkness upon darkness. Lying half-conscious and half-drained, roped to the iron bedframe. And night after night LaRouge descended upon him, and drank him nearly to death, and afterward cooed in his ear and traced circles upon his chest with fingernails dark with graveyard dirt.

"This is how it happens," said Corporal Nibbett, the legless Confederate who had actually lost his limbs *after* he'd become infected with vampirism. Out on a battlefield with the others, going from throat to throat in the settling dusk…and then the cannons had opened up and the balls had come sizzling in, and… "Lopped my legs off, quick as you please," Nibbett had said, his seamed and chalky face grinning in the candlelight. The corporal—an ex-blacksmith from Georgia—came down sometimes, slithering himself along the stairs and then the dirt, to talk awhile in the presence of the gentleman captain from Alabama. "Just felt a burnin', and it was over. Ain't gonna grow 'em back, though. Wish I could. But done is done, I reckon."

In his state of blood-drained shock, the gentleman captain from Alabama could not answer.

"How goes old Bobby Lee?" Nibbett asked. And, to the silence, replied, "Gonna lick them Yanks yet. But ya know…don't matter much, now. Patrick and Gordy… they's both Yanks. Lil' Priss, she's a Yank. Campfollower. No, don't matter much, now." He slapped the stub of a leg. "Boy howdy, we're all on the same damned side now, ain't we? Fightin' again' *them*. You know. Them who's wantin' us to *die*. Oh, it's a war all right. Been goin' on a

long time, but most don't know it. Us agin' them. As old
as time, that's what LaRouge says. Oh, she's likin' you,
Cap'n. Say she was a woman of some wealth, back a ways."
He leaned forward, his red-centered eyes ashine. "Some of
them older ones, they call her *Queen* LaRouge. She speaks
French. Seems like that's the right language for a queen to
be speakin'. Damn, I am gettin' me some hungry. It just
falls on you. Just troubles you, and you got to have it." His
dirty right hand crawled like a spider upon Lawson's chest.
"Feel that heart beatin', movin' that blood. Ohhhh...yessir.
I can smell that sure as I used to smell Maudie's bacon a'-
fryin' in the mornin'. You got yourself some *holes* in that
neck, Cap'n! She's been workin' you somethin' *good*! Oh,
I smell that blood, yessir. Smell that *life*. Lemme just take
a lick a' that, one lil' ole lick!"

The gentleman captain from Alabama could not
refuse.

"This is how it happens," Nibbett had said, close to
Lawson's ear. "You think you're in a bad dream. You think
all is lost. She drinks the blood out of you...slow, slow...
and everytime she drinks from you it takes you closer. Oh,
you won't believe what you can do, when she gets done
with you. When she *turns* you. From bein' a blood-puppet
to bein' strong and fast, and never gettin' no older. And
the things you *know*, and the things you can *see*...well, it's
all revelations. Now look at me, a'sittin' here with no legs.
I ought to be dead by now, but I ain't. Near 'bout *can't*

die. Oh, I hear the older ones say they's ways, but...I hear that heart beatin', Cap'n. You are a strong young horse, ain't you? Another lil' lick...just one. If LaRouge saw me doin' that...well, she would tear me to pieces and that would finish me. Cut my head off, I reckon that would do it. See, we don't have blood no more. Not like you. The older ones call it *ichor*. I don't understand it all, but that's what makes us different. *Better.* You'll see. You'll feel it in you, and you'll know. Only thing is...I used to like the mornin' sun so much. Used to like to watch it rise over the field and burn the mist off. Now..." He shrugged his thin shoulders. "Ain't nothin'," he said.

Lawson slept in his root cellar prison, and awakened, and slept. He was aware of figures hovering around him, curious at his progress from human into one of them. He was aware of the woman in red over him, and her face contorting as she opened her mouth wide and wider still and the curved fangs slid out.

"Gonna be turned soon," said Nibbett, sitting next to the pallid captain on one of his many visits. "Two or three more times oughta do it. Drink you down to nothin' so's you can be filled up again. Feel them fangs start to grow, they'll just slide out when you need 'em. Then we'll take you huntin'. Lots of good game 'round here, the two-legged kind. You go in so fast, they never know what hits 'em. You'll learn, Cap'n. Then you'll see what it's like to be one of us, and you'll know them revelations."

Trevor Lawson had looked up into Nibbett's face, there in the light of the single candle, and forced the words from his bleached lips. "Human. Will I...ever be human again?"

"Not a blood-puppet no more, no. Not after you're full turned." Nibbett had frowned. "Well...there's a way, I hear...but you won't want to. After you feel and see and you *are*, you won't care to go back. Only way...is to drink the ichor from the one who's turned you. Drink it all down. Then you go back to what you were, and you *age*. Hell, some of 'em would turn to dust, if that was to happen. Ain't gonna be a thought in your head though. All that goes away. You'll see. Trust an ol' rebel, Cap'n. Once you get turned...you ain't ever gonna want to go back."

Lawson came back from memory, and from sleep. He felt the sun sinking, felt the world cooling toward night. His time. When he winnowed out of the black curtains he found Ann Kingsley still in her boat, which she'd also roped to a cypress. She was bleary-eyed and bug-bitten, had obviously also been sleeping, and she held her pistol on him.

The sun was almost gone. The stars were coming out, and the night creatures of the swamp were awakening. Lawson removed his dark-tinted goggles. He stretched his body and removed himself from the rest of his protective shroud.

"I'm ready," he said. "Can you keep up with me?"

"I can."

He doubted it, but they didn't have very far to go, according to McGuire's map. The torch had burned itself out; no need to relight it, because they knew he was coming. "All right," he told her, as he got the rope free and pulled it back into his skiff. He took up the oars. "Follow me."

Into what? he wondered. Certain destruction? What was he going to do about her? Cast his Eye and make her go back? It wasn't that simple. The spell didn't last that long, and not over distance. He was responsible for her life now too, it seemed.

"Interesting choice of a career for yourself," he told her. "How did the daughter of a wealthy politician become a trick shot artist working for Remington?"

"I've always been a good shot," she answered after a short pause. "I wasn't raised to be fancy. I was raised to take care of myself, and to be…quick to act and determined, when I have to be. Which is why I'm here. Also, I suppose…I like challenges."

Lawson thought, as he rowed ahead of her and she followed, that he owed her something. She had come this far and she was ready to fight for the life of her sister, but she didn't know what she was getting into. Maybe it was time to break his silence and tell her.

He let the boat drift until she caught up beside him. The sickle moon was rising over the treetops, and the branches of trees reached out on all sides over the water. The drone of the swamp had just begun.

Lawson paused to light a cigar. He blew a plume of smoke, and through it he said, "For your information, and it will certainly be a challenge to your belief...I am a vampire, Miss Kingsley, and you are following me into the world of the Dark Society."

Eight.

MISS KINGSLEY SAID NOTHING. THE water hissed around her oars.

"A vampire," Lawson repeated. "Do you know what that is? A creature no longer human? Well, in my case... partly so. I am hanging on to what I was, as hard as I can. That means drinking animal blood instead of human blood. I can't digest very much else. I can't bear very much sunlight, which is why I sleep during the day protected in my shroud. I am between worlds, let us say. Are you still with me?"

Miss Kingsley still said nothing. Both their boats drifted under the horned moon.

"I was wounded on the battlefield at Shiloh on the sixth of April, 1862," Lawson went on, easily, as if he

were talking about the smells of wild honeysuckle or
the muck of the mire. "A feast of vampires caught me.
I was taken to where they lived. *Existed*," he corrected.
"A female who called herself LaRouge turned me into
one of them, over a period of time. I found out from
one of the others that if you can drain the ichor—the
vampiric fluid—from the creature who turned you,
you may become human again. Whether that's true or
not, I don't know. He didn't either. When they took
me out hunting the first time, I had to kill one of them
to get away. His name was Nibbett, and I cut his head
off with a butcher knife in a farmhouse. It was not
a pretty scene. They came after me, of course. They
were *fast*. But I was desperate, and I was determined,
and I jumped from a bridge into a river and I was gone.
After that...a horror story. A story of a hungry creature,
in agony at what he was becoming. Then he became
a starving creature, until he began to rip the throats
out of cattle and swine from farm to farm. That will
keep you alive, he found out, but you begin to weaken
without the human blood. You begin to...dwindle. But
Nibbett was right about the revelations." Lawson looked
up beyond the treetops at the stars, and saw them blue
and burning and beautiful as no human eye could ever
behold. He saw the swirls of the evening breeze like
the cool green phosphoresence of ocean waves. He saw
the azure shine of the eyes of animals peering back at

him from the underbrush on either side of the channel, and looking into the face of Ann Kingsley in the moon-touched dark he could see her as clearly as if the lamp of the heavens was turned directly upon her expression of combined solemnity and incredulity.

"I have become an adventurer for my livelihood," Lawson continued. "I will go where I am summoned, and do the task I am asked to do, for payment. I choose who I will work for, and why. It all becomes night work, eventually. I have hunted and brought to bay the killers of a judge in Texas. I have bested a gunfighter in Wyoming who terrorized a town for extortion money. I have tracked three escaped convicts and their hostages through the snow in North Dakota. I have brought a cunning fox of a blackmailer to justice in San Francisco, and in Chicago I put an end to a maniac who lured young women and rewarded their love with a razor blade. And in all that time and in those places and many more, I looked for signs of the Dark Society's presence. I searched for news of the drained bodies they would leave behind, and I searched the places I thought they might be hiding. Several times I found them by following their trails, and we had our battles. I've killed quite a few, and they've nearly killed me. By then they knew what I wanted. Once—last March in Kansas City—I even found LaRouge. She was cleaned-up and quite beautiful. I got close enough in a saloon to touch her, and she looked into my face with fear. Her horde closed in on me and tried to tear me to pieces. I had to get away for my life...such as it is. But she fears me because she knows what I desire, and that I won't give up. And she is right." Lawson punctuated this with a slow spool of smoke and a tense smile through it. "So this Christian Melchoir has taken your sister on the command of LaRouge," Lawson said. "To bring me to them, in a place they control. They knew I would have to come, because *she* might be there." He regarded the cigar's burning tip. "If she might be there...any chance at all...I have to risk the trap. And it *will* be a trap, Miss Kingsley. Your sister may not be fully human any longer. She may have been turned. Oh... and the six hundred and sixty six dollars in gold coins?" Lawson tapped one of the saddlebags with a boot. "The Number of the Beast in the Book Of Revelations. I suppose that in their opinion, *I* am the Beast. The traitor who wishes to destroy them...so it's fitting they should demand I bring that amount into their midst. They have little need for the gold; they want me...my ichor, my flesh, my bones, my body ripped into a hundred thousand pieces and scattered to burn in the noonday sun." He slid the cigar back into his mouth and sat staring at Ann without expression. "I'm sure you have questions," he said.

Ann Kingsley lifted her pistol, cocked it and took aim at Lawson's head. Her eyes had become very wide.

Lawson smoked his cigar with his shrinking lungs and calmly surveyed the scene. "Do you know," he said, "why I have two guns?"

She didn't reply. Her hand was shaking, just a little bit.

"The Colt on the right with the rosewood grip is to defend myself against humans. It's usually loaded with regular lead slugs. But this Colt on my left, with the grip of bone…is to defend myself against my own breed. It's loaded with bullets of pure silver, blessed with holy water by a priest friend of mine. The effect of this bullet, fired into a vampire's skull, is to burn the creature's body and reduce it to a fine ash. Why this works, I do not know, but my friend wished me to use it due to some experiences he had." Lawson shrugged. "I can tell you that it works very well. Before I left St. Benadicta I loaded both .44s with the silver bullets. I also carry a derringer with the same silver-and-holy-water slugs. Again…it works. And thankful I am that it does, because I would likely be dead by now." He tapped ashes into the water, as both his boat and Ann's drifted southward with a slow current. "*Fully* dead," he added. "That is not my plan."

Ann Kingsley spoke. Her voice sounded ravaged.

"You are insane," she said.

Lawson answered, "The lead bullets from your .44 won't kill them, but they don't like to be wounded or have a bone broken. It hurts them, for a short time. Human blood helps them regenerate any injury. Except a severed arm or leg," he added, thinking of Nibbett. Though if Nibbett had lived long enough and drank enough of the human elixir, even those might have regrown in some misshapen form or fashion. "I carry extra silver bullets in my holster and in my saddlebags. I'll give you some, if you like."

"Madness," Ann whispered.

Lawson sensed it before it happened. Something was out there, about shoulder-high, over the channel. He put his hand out and touched the rusted chain that hung from tree-to-tree. Then the bells hidden in the trees rang. There were about six of them, a couple small and high-pitched, the others more of a funeral tone. The sound of the bells echoed off along the passage.

Lawson lifted the chain over his head so both his skiff and Ann's could glide under. "We've just announced ourselves," he said quietly. "What I've told you is the truth. The Dark Society is the underworld of vampires and... other creatures. They have existed for a very long time. You should go back, Ann. Leave this to me." He paused, hoping for a breakthrough. "What's your decision?"

She didn't answer for a few seconds. Lawson thought she may have lost her voice. Then: "I'm going to save my sister, and you may be insane but I am not."

"All right." Lawson let the chain drop when Ann's skiff had cleared it. They continued to drift. He considered showing her his fangs. In truth, the warm blood smell of her was working on him. Best to keep the fangs in their sockets, he decided. If she wanted to go into what was ahead…so be it.

"Row," he told her, as he picked up his oars and began. She put her pistol aside, and followed him.

In another few minutes they heard distant music.

It was the music of fiddles and cellos, punctuated by the rattle and bang of tambourines. It was coming from around the next bend, where willow trees drooped into the water and cypress roots thrust from the muddy earth. Lawson kept rowing, and to her credit the young woman did not falter. "I believe we've reached Nocturne," Lawson said, as they rounded the bend and saw what lay before them.

The upper floors of what must have been magnificent mansions loomed from the swamp. Gabled roofs were covered with moss and thick stone columns descended into the mire. The high steeple of a church stood beyond these structures, crooked like a dunce's cap that had been knocked awry. At its summit was a Cross that seemed to be about to fall from its prominence into the despair at its bottom. Dark and glassless windows observed the world. Yet not all the windows of these mansions were dark. One that showed two floors above the surface of hundreds of waterlillies was lighted by candles, and it was from this remnant of Nocturne's glory that the music wafted. Like the church steeple, the house itself was a little crooked, as if it had shifted on its uncertain foundations. Cracks in the lichen-blotched walls had been filled in by thick vines that might well be holding the house together. Several boats, including a larger vessel that looked like some kind of logger's workcraft with a barracks aboard, were roped to the mansion's columns. It occurred to Lawson that there was probably some swamp town other than St. Benadicta the vampires had come through, to get these boats and spirit Eva Kingsley down. Most likely they had feasted on the inhabitants of that town and either left it for the vultures or turned whomever it pleased them to.

It was merry music. The Dark Society was having a party this night.

He suspected he would be the guest of honor, and also the party favor.

He heard Ann give a quiet gasp, and he thought that she was beginning to realize what realm she had indeed entered.

"I'll take those bullets," she said.

Lawson opened one of his saddlebags, got out the box of silver slugs that Father Deale procured for him from a bullet maker in West New Orleans, and gave Ann a handful. He winced slightly. "Starting to burn my fingers," he explained. Ann quickly unloaded her lead slugs and replaced them with the deadly silver angels. The remainder went into the ammo loops of her holster.

"Not that I believe you," she told him. "I'm not saying that."

"Of course," he replied. He began rowing again and she followed. He aimed his boat through the mass of waterlillies toward the candlelit mansion, and now he saw that the way in was through a large window of the second floor. Part of it had been broken away to allow the entrance of more small boats, which were moored within. Candlelight from a huge overhead chandelier glinted off the water that had flooded the house, and Lawson saw upon the walls the dark stains and patterns of rot. A staircase led up from the murky depths to the floor above. The music was bright and festive. Figures passed by the windows of the third floor, some holding burning tapers.

Lawson rowed his skiff through the opening into the diseased mansion, and after a short hesitation to confirm her courage the young woman rowed in after him.

Lawson looked up the staircase. It opened into a larger chamber above. He took his saddlebags, got out of his boat and stepped onto the nearest and dryest riser, which sagged under his weight. He helped Ann out. They stood on the rotten stairs peering up. Ann's Remington was gripped in her hand. Lawson was ready to draw a pistol at any second.

A figure holding a double-wicked candleabra came through the doorway and stood at the top of the stairs.

It was a girl maybe sixteen or seventeen years old—at least in appearance...wearing a moldy green gown. She had long blonde hair and an attractive oval face and she smiled at them as if they were precious to her. "Come up!" she urged. "Oh, do come up!"

Lawson spent a moment tying their boats to the bannister. He felt Ann shiver at his side. He looked into her face and felt the warmth of her blood pulling at him; he could almost hear her heartbeat, and the rush of the delicious fluid through her veins. "Listen to me," he said tersely. "Stay beside me. If one gets too close, shoot it in the head...whatever it looks like: man, woman or child."

"Ya'll come on up here this *instant*!" said the young girl, with a born-to-the-plantation petulance. And then, to whomever was beyond the chamber's entrance: "He's brought us a pretty!"

"Oh...my God..." Ann whispered.

Too late for that, Lawson thought. Way damned too late.

For the vampire gunslinger and his pretty, it was time to join the party. He started up the rotten staircase, which trembled beneath him. Ann got herself moving, and together they ascended toward the gathering.

Nine.

"WE'VE BEEN WAITIN' FOR *YOU!*" said the blonde female with a fierce grin, as Lawson and Ann reached the top of the stairs. At closer range, her eyes were sunken in and glinted with red in the candlelight and the front of her dress was dark with dried blood. Lawson could feel Ann shrinking back.

"Steady," he told her, as much for himself as anyone. They were both a long way from home.

The music was becoming more frantic and ragged. Within the chamber that stood before them, candles burning on wall sconces illuminated the figures at this demonic festival, their shadows thrown large upon the moldy green walls. To the tune of vampire musicians

playing two fiddles, a bass violin and a pair of tambourines, the gathering danced and whirled across
the rot-stained boards, some moving so fast they were
only ghostly blurs. By Lawson's quick count, there
were between thirty and forty creatures of the night
at this fandango. There was nearly an equality of men
and women of various ages in appearance, yet Lawson
knew appearances could be deceiving in this regard.
A few pallid children clung to the legs of what might
be their mothers, indicating a sorry and sad history
for that particular family. The women in their dirty
gowns twirled and the men in their mud-stained suits
pranced back and forth. Eyes that sparked red in the
light of the flickering tapers were aimed quickly in
the direction of Lawson and his charge, and just as
quickly averted.

The young blonde vampire leaned forward to sniff
Ann's hair. Ann cringed away with a start and brought
her six up into firing position. The girl laughed and
snatched the dark green jockey's cap from Ann's head.
Putting it on her own head, the less-than-human creature darted away to join the dancers, the speed of her
departure blowing the tapers dead in her candleabra.

"I neglected to tell you," said Lawson, "how fast
they...we...are. Take a good long look. You may never see
such a sight again." If you live after seeing this one, he
thought grimly.

The music urged the vampire dancers to further exertions. As they spun around the chamber, in which mounted upon the walls were rotten gray tapestries that had become part of the decor of swamp decay and twisted vines that had burst their way through from the outside, they became almost indistinguishable from each other, their blood-fed bodies merging one with another in the blurring of their motion.

Lawson smoked his cigar and watched the dancers. He was aware that at the center of the chamber, and at the center of the ring of bodies, was a single chair. And in that chair was roped the body of a woman, dressed in dirty clothes, with a black hood over her head. The head was slumped forward, the body slack.

"Is that…Eva?" Ann whispered. "*Dead?*"

"I don't know," Lawson answered, though he expected the worst. The Dark Society was not going to allow any of them to walk out of here.

The blonde female vampire who wore Ann's cap suddenly came out of the ring, grinning and whirling around and around like a human top. She got up close to Ann and stopped her motion, and she smelled Ann's hair and neck and in the next instant her body shivered with desire and her mouth opened wide. Her lower jaw unhinged, the fangs slid out and her eyes of cornflower blue flamed with bloodneed as she gripped the back of Ann's neck and thrust her mouth toward the woman's throat.

Before Ann could react, Lawson shot the creature in the side of her head. The noise of the shot made the music abruptly skreech to a halt and the ring of dancers froze in their steps. As the blonde vampire staggered back, her mouth open in an O of shock and her body already beginning to break apart and burn from the inside out, Lawson calmly plucked the jockey's cap from the thing's head. He gave it to Ann, and said, "Ready your six, but don't move."

The vampire's long blonde hair caught fire and sizzled away in a matter of seconds. Her face rippled and turned black as it burned. She clutched at her throat as if recalling the moment of her turning, and as she spun around and around in a mad and agonized parody of the dance her eyes sank inward and burst into black pools that bubbled and smoked before they became dried craters, her burned facial features imploded, and her head began to wither like a grape left out in the blazing sun. From the ruin of the mouth and the collapsing throat came a piercing scream of rage. Lawson had heard such a scream before, but he knew this sight and this sound must be nearly knocking Ann to her knees. With the passage of four more seconds, an empty green gown stained dark with old blood fell upon a pile of ashes and a pair of ashy brown shoes.

Silence ruled.

It was broken by someone clapping.

"Impressive!" said a man from amid the ring. "Im...
pressive!" He continued clapping as he came forward,
easily, without fear, from the throng. "I had heard you
had a weapon that...shall we say...gave you an advantage,
but *this*...ah, quite a show!"

"Thank you," Lawson replied. He kept his drawn
Colt, the one with the grip of yellow bone, ready at his
side. "Would you like to see another example of it?"

"No need! Let's just call it a nice magic trick, eh?"
He stopped and spread his arms wide. "Well, brother
Lawson...how do you like my town?"

"A little damp," said Lawson. "A little musty. I think
it's just a matter of time before it slides into the swamp."

"True," Christian Melchoir replied. He frowned, and
with a toe of a black boot prodded at the empty green
gown and the ashes of a dead vampire. "Painfully true.
But it won't happen this night! This night...we celebrate!"

"Celebrate what?"

"Your homecoming. Your chance to rejoin your
tribe, sir. And look, you've brought us a peace offering.
Musicians!" Melchoir turned toward them. "Please keep
playing! Everyone, dance as you like! We are here to bring
brother Lawson back into our fold, so please...make him
feel welcome!" As the musicians began scratching out a
tune again, Melchoir grinned at his new guests. "Did you
tell this blood-puppet everything? Did you *prepare* her?
Oh, that must have been quite the moment!"

Lawson was content to say nothing and smoke his cigar. He was taking stock of Christian Melchoir. The man was tall and lean and dressed in a swamp-stained gray suit with a dark blue shirt and a lighter blue paisley waistcoat. He appeared to be about twenty-five years old, his pale face smooth and unlined. He had curly black hair and a high-cheekboned face with a long angular nose and a cleft in his chin. His grin was ferocious and hungry, his eyes cool gray under gracefully-arched eyebrows. He gazed from Lawson to Ann and back again, as a few of the vampires continued their dance around the woman in the chair and the others watched the confrontation with a nervous interest, for the sudden extermination of the blonde vampire had served to focus their attention on a small item of mortality they had forgotten about in their present condition.

"Well," said Lawson, as he blew smoke into the steamy air. "I've come to pay you the ransom you requested. First I want to see Eva's face."

"We'll get to that, if you insist upon it."

"I want Eva back." Ann aimed her Remington at Melchoir's head. The gun was miraculously steady, though her voice was certainly not. "I want her untied *now*."

"Tell your pretty," said Melchoir with a fixed smile, "that she does not give orders here. And please lower that gun before anyone else is damaged." He motioned toward someone amid the watchers. A bald, big-shouldered and barrel-chested vampire in a filthy white shirt and black trousers walked a few steps to Eva's side, slid a derringer from his pocket and placed the little pistol's barrel against her right temple. The body stirred and the head gave a startled jerk.

"She has come to no harm *yet*," Melchoir went on. "We want *you*, Lawson. Of course you know that. Very brave of you to come here, but why bring a blood-puppet?"

"She's the girl's sister. I couldn't stop her."

"Not so good with the powers of persuasion then, are you?" Melchoir came forward two more paces before he stopped again, warily eyeing Ann's six-shooter and Lawson's Colts, the one in his hand and the other still holstered. "We have thirty-eight of us here tonight," he offered. "Um...pardon me, thirty-seven now. Do you have that many of those magic bullets in your guns? I don't think so. You can destroy some of us, surely. But..." He opened his mouth wide to show his fangs, which were particularly large and curved. "These will win," he said when the fangs had slid back into their sockets again. "Eventually, they will win everything."

"First you built a town that slid into the muck. Now you want to build a world?"

"We want to keep our Society alive and...healthy, so to speak. That means...well, you *know* what it means."

Lawson did. It meant the blood hunts by night and the destruction of one farmhouse family after another...

and the destruction of one small town after another...
and more and more, until...when?...the end of time? He
spewed out a slow crawl of smoke. "That's where you
and I differ," he said. He took stock of the chamberful of
vampires, as the music continued to play and the dancers
ringed around the girl in the chair. There were too many
to shoot; even as fast as he was, he couldn't kill them all.
He thought: *If you're gonna jump into that fryin' pan...*

"My town," said Melchoir. "Our world. You can still be
part of it, Lawson. There's no need for your dubious quest."

"There's a need."

Melchoir gave a slight and menacing smile that
quickly faded. "You can't go back. You can only go forward, as what you are. Don't you understand that yet?"

"I understand I'm not like *you* yet. Before I get there,
I'll—"

"Shoot yourself with one of those bullets?" Melchoir
came another two paces nearer. Lawson noted that two
vampires—an older, rugged-looking man and a young
dark-haired woman—were edging closer on the left, and
on the right were two young males, also getting closer.
All of them wore filthy clothes stained with the gore of
many victims. "Shouldn't you do that now, then, and
save yourself some time?"

"I'll wait," said Lawson. Beside him, Ann still held
the six-shooter aimed at Melchoir, though she was also
aware of the four creatures converging on them.

"My father used to say that to me." Melchoir's face had become tight, his cheekbones standing out in relief in the pallid, yellowish flesh. "In that great big white house on the river. He used to say...'Christian, you should shoot yourself now and save yourself some time'. Wasn't that so very kind of him? Well...I showed him what I was made of. I stood up to him. Many times I did. And when he said I was a failure and I would always be a failure, I said I would show him I could not only beat him to the ground in the business...but I would do it from a town I had built from impossible earth. Nocturne, my night song. My great creation." The tight face tried to smile, but it was only a strained half-smile and it was terribly ugly. "You have come home, Lawson. We want to embrace you."

"I'm sure you do," said Lawson, who watched the four vampires coming ever nearer. Lawson decided to wait no longer. He shot one of the two young males in the head, and as the music halted again and the throng watched in horrified fascination the creature burned away in his nasty clothes and fell to ashes. On the left, the older male vampire propelled itself forward with incredible speed. Ann fired a shot at the thing but put a hole only in the far wall because the monster had become nearly invisible. As it fell upon Ann and its fangs slid out toward her throat, Lawson shot it just above the left eye and it gave a high-pitched shriek and staggered back, its face already darkening and beginning to ripple and implode.

"Everyone stay calm," said Christian Melchoir, as ashes flew about the chamber and more dirty and blood-stained clothes littered the floor.

Lawson threw one of his saddlebags at Melchoir's feet. "Your payment in gold is there. Count it if you please, it's in a leather pouch. We're taking Eva Kingsley, and we're leaving."

"Are you, now?"

Lawson clenched the cigar between his teeth, the Colt with the bone handle gripped in his right hand. "We are. Move aside."

Melchoir lifted his hands, and moved aside.

"Walk with me," Lawson quietly told Ann. "Don't stumble. Don't fall." It was the advice he would have given anyone who found themselves in a snakepit. He moved forward and she went with him as close as a second skin.

"You are wrong to be hunting LaRouge," Melchoir said as they passed him. "She doesn't like it. None of us like the fact that you are murdering your own kind. She demands that you cease your pointless wanderings and fully join us, or you will have to be destroyed."

Lawson said nothing. He and Ann were nearing the circle.

"Let them pass," said Melchoir, and they opened a place for Lawson and Ann to enter. Once they were within the circle, it closed again. The big vampire with the derringer moved to one side, and Lawson thought he would have to kill this one next.

Ann rushed to her sister. The body in the chair trembled, as if with anticipation.

Lawson said, *"Wait."* The sound of his voice stopped Ann from touching the black hood. He came over beside her, and when he was there the figure in the chair began to smoothly stand up and the ropes that had been loosely tied but not knotted fell away and the slim hands rose up to remove the black hood, and there...

...there stood before him the creature with waves of black hair and the beautiful face of a fallen angel. She was still regal in her evil; she still wore it grandly and proudly, though this night she did not wear crimson yet her black eyes held crimson in their depths like pools of flame.

"Hello, Trevor," LaRouge whispered, smiling faintly as she glided toward him. "I think you've been looking for me?"

Ten.

LAWSON'S FIRST IMPULSE WAS TO lift his gun to her head...but he did not, for he *could* not. She was his death-in-life and his life-in-death, and he could not send her whirling away into fire and ash. Not, at least, until he had drained her black ichor...

"My sister!" Ann's voice was frantic. "Where's my sister?"

"Turned," said Christian Melchior, who had come into the circle at their back. "And turned *out*. Lawson... you had to know we weren't going to give her over to you. You came here hoping to find LaRouge. Isn't that true? And *why*? To destroy her? Or to join with her?"

Lawson stood his ground as LaRouge's face neared his. Her hand came out and stroked his cheek. "Beautiful boy," she whispered. "Never aging. Strong and fierce, forever. Living wild and free. You have been searching for me, not because you desire to kill me, *non*." Her fingers moved across his lips. "Because you desire *me*," she said. "There is no going back to what you were. That is a foolish dream, and not your destiny." Her tongue, black as a serpent's spine, came out and licked along his jawline. "Your destiny is here with us, Trevor. With *me*. I am fascinated by your fight against what you are, and what you will become. I've never known anyone like you. But you have been so… so *disobedient*. So *naughty*. Killing your own kind, and *why*? You are no longer human, Trevor. Accept that. It will be so much better."

Lawson managed to speak, with an effort. "I am… still human. I *am*."

"No, you are not," she whispered in his ear. "You are much more than human. And in time…when you give yourself fully over…you will learn to be a *god*."

A gun was cocked.

The barrel of a Remington pistol was placed against LaRouge's head.

Slowly, as if enmeshed in the most hideous dream, Lawson reached up and pushed the barrel away.

LaRouge smiled.

"We will turn this one together," she told him. "Or would you rather kill her now? I'll let you decide. But please make a quick decision, because I am very hungry."

Lawson felt the conflicting tides move within him. He smelled the blood of ages on LaRouge's breath. He smelled the ruination of souls and the dirt of the grave. A *god*, he thought. Able to live forever, strong and fierce. Forever young, at least in appearance…forever wild and free.

She was right there, in front of him, and she was offering him eternity as she knew it to be.

With a slow hand he unbuttoned his black coat.

Then he unbuttoned his crimson waistcoat.

With the burning end of his Marsh-Wheeling he lit the end of the fuse that was revealed. The fuse was connected to eight sticks of dynamite, four on each side, in a small leather harness that hung around his neck and against his shirt. It was what he'd asked Father Deale to procure for him, before he left New Orleans. He could image the priest asking to buy eight sticks of dynamite from a supplier. But Father Deale was nothing if not persuasive, and the items had been waiting for him in a box at the front desk.

The fuse sparked and sizzled.

LaRouge looked at it, her eyes widening. There was enough explosive to blow her and every creature in this chamber to pieces that could never, ever find their way back together again.

Lawson said, "I came here plenty oiled up."

"*What?*" LaRouge whispered, rage beginning to surface in her voice.

He looked at Ann.

"Get out," he said, and handed her the second Colt. "However you can."

Then Lawson grabbed hold of LaRouge, pinning her arms at her sides, and in that instant when all the vampires of the Dark Society were stunned by a man who had chosen death over undeath, he let his own rage rise up from the depths. His mouth opened, the lower jaw unhinged and the fangs slid out, and he bit into LaRouge's throat where the ichor ran black and thick. He tasted her, the most bitter wine he had ever sipped, and then he drank her in great swallows. By his estimation he had less than a minute before the fuse burned to the first stick.

Many things happened at once, in the wake of this shock. LaRouge fought wildly. She was strong, and as she hissed and struggled she and Lawson staggered left and right as if locked in their own dance. Some of the vampires drew back and others rushed forward. Ann shot the burly bald vampire in the head, aimed a shot at Melchoir and missed because he was already a moving blur advancing on her. Another shot missed again, even at a range of only a few feet, and then Ann was running for the nearest window. An arm caught her around the neck and pulled her back, and as she twisted to face her attacker she saw it was not Melchoir but a young boy who might have been sixteen years old, his tangled hair the color of sawdust, his face bony and his eyes aflame. Dried blood caked the front of his blue-checked shirt. His fangs strained for her throat, and she put the Remington up under his chin and fired into his head the fifth of her six silver angels in that cylinder.

Melchoir had abandoned his attack on Ann Kingsley for bigger game.

He hit Lawson like a steam engine. In spite of that, Lawson held onto LaRouge and his gun and continued to drink, as the fuse burned down and the seconds ticked past and LaRouge tried to get her arms up to throw him aside or plunge her claws into his eyes but she could not.

As the vampires came at Ann with tremendous speed, she fired the last of her Remington's ammunition into their midst and then opened up with the Colt. Two of them were hit and began to sizzle and break apart, which made the others draw back. Ashes flew in the flickering yellow light, but there were too many. The window was at Ann's back; she was about to jump, and then she froze as she witnessed a transformation from a nightmare world.

Christian Melchoir was changing. His body color darkened, like that of a chameleon on a gray rock. His skin rippled into scales. His forehead thickened, his jaw lengthened, his hands became knotty claws. Something twitched and moved at his back, under his gray suit coat. His body became thickly muscular in a span of seconds. With the ripping of cloth two ebony wings burst from beneath his shirt and waistcoat and suit coat, and unfolding they made him appear to be a huge gnarled and muscular bat, even as his head seemed to sink into his shoulders and his face became animalish, his mouth opening and the fangs tearing at the air.

She fired a silver angel at him, but he was already gone.

Melchoir hit Lawson with a force that lifted the vampire gunslinger off his feet and tore him away from LaRouge, leaving grooves in her flesh that leaked the ink-black ichor. He lost his hold on his pistol and it skidded away across the planks. LaRouge staggered back as Melchoir's claws closed around Lawson's shoulders and bit into the flesh, and just that quickly the bat-creature's wings beat the air and thrust both of them through a window on the other side of the room, out of the ruined mansion and into the night before Ann could take aim again.

LaRouge's burning gaze fell upon Ann Kingsley.

Ann lifted the Colt to fire. She was aware of blurred shapes coming at her from all sides, aware that she could get off one shot before the others took her.

She remembered Lawson saying, as if pleading it to himself, *I am still human. I am.*

Ann turned to the left and shot a thin, ragged and gray-haired female vampire who'd been just about to reach her. The woman gave a shrill cry of what might have been terror as she blackened and broke apart, her eyes bursting like blisters and a gout of blue fire coming from her mouth.

Ann had an instant to see LaRouge advancing on her, grinning like a death's-head, and then Ann turned and jumped through the window into the swamp below.

In the air over Nocturne, Lawson twisted his body around to grab hold of the shape that Christian Melchoir had shifted himself into. The fuse was still sizzling; maybe he had twenty seconds. Melchoir tried to sling Lawson downward, the ebony wings beating furiously, but Lawson hung on. They spun in a mad circle, another crazed dance in midair. Lawson made an attempt to get his body up onto Melchoir's shoulders, but the wings beat at him and the creature was too strong.

Lawson's back slammed into something that nearly broke his spine. Melchoir had crashed him into the church's steeple. The impact made the crooked Cross topple from its mount into the water thirty feet below. Melchoir pulled him back again, and once more rammed Lawson into the steeple with a force that cracked ribs and made the gunslinger cry out with pain. The third time Lawson was crashed against the steeple, a clawed hand reached down and crushed out the burning fuse. Lawson grasped hold of the steeple's roof tiles and strained for breath as the bat-creature in Melchoir's clothes hovered before him in triumph, its wings thrashing the air.

"My town," came the ragged, otherworldly voice from the distorted vocal cords. "Our world."

"Wrong," Lawson rasped, his back and ribs pulsing with pain. "You're about to leave...both of them." As he hung onto the steeple with one arm, he lifted the pearl-handled derringer he'd taken from its pocket inside his coat.

Lawson fired a silver bullet into the creature's head just below the right eye. The shot echoed out into the night.

Melchoir's wings drew him backward. As the body convulsed and the red fissures broke open and the vampire's life essence was destroyed by the silver and the holy water, one wing collapsed while the other continued to beat, which put Melchoir in a circle going around and around the steeple. Lawson lay back, nearly exhausted, the bitter taste of LaRouge's ichor in his mouth and the veins of his body itching as if coming back to life, his face feverish, his nerves on fire.

He watched Christian Melchoir burn. Watched the face collapse inward. The eyes remained fixed upon him, it seemed, until they burst and ran in rivulets down the cheeks. The mouth was open in a soundless oath of surprise. Lawson watched the chest and arms and back shrivel, watched the wings crumble to ash and fall away, and then the smoking torso and the misshapen head still with a mat of crisped hair turned to ashes, and all that was left of the creator of Nocturne and the savior of the creature called LaRouge fell into the swamp along with his clothing.

Lawson listened.

There was no more music here.

He could still see candlelight in the mansion beyond. If Ann had been taken...

He didn't wish to think about that. He didn't wish to think. He had lost his prized Stetson, which made him a little angry. He had one more cigar, and luckily this had survived being fully crushed. He had several more friction matches. He decided he would have a smoke, if he could risk blowing up his dynamite waistcoat. It was a risk worth taking. He was still alive; he meant to stay that way, as long as he could, but he did enjoy a good cigar. His movements were slow and labored, but at least he *could* move.

Yes, there was music, after all.

The sound of the swamp rose up to him. The sound of frogs and crickets, of birds and 'gators, of life in every puddle and pond and knothole and leaf.

Nothing came after him. He lay against the crooked dunce-cap steeple and smoked his cigar and relished for a moment his safety. He could see the blue shimmer of the stars. He could also see, to the east, the faint glow of the sunrise.

Lawson smiled grimly. Caught on a church steeple, with maybe three or four broken ribs and a spine that had nearly been snapped. Caught here with the sun coming up and eight sticks of dynamite on his chest. Father Deale would get a good laugh out of this one.

There was still enough fuse left to blow himself up, if he pleased. There was one more silver bullet in the derringer. He could go that way too, if he wished.

He would think about that, he decided, when he finished his cigar. And maybe he would watch the sun rise, as well. Burn his eyes out with its beauty, this last time.

He heard a distant voice, calling "Christian? Christian?"

It was a woman's voice, accented with French. *Her* voice. "Christian?" she called, a third time. But no one answered, and LaRouge ceased calling because she had heard the shot and must've known he was dead.

Would they leave the party now? Lawson wondered. Get in their boats and go away? And go where? Or would they hide here in the daylight and leave when the sun sank again? He could imagine them going back in a little armada to whatever swamp town they'd conquered and consumed, and from there out into all points of the compass, out into the Big Country with all it promised for the vampire, out into the world of ordinary mortals and unsuspecting humans who knew nothing of the Dark Society and so were unprepared when they came in the night.

After awhile a man called for Christian, again from the distance. And once more, with a little chill of fear in the voice: "*Christian?*"

He is not here, Lawson thought. He is no longer among you. But I am still here, and I am not leaving yet.

Lawson watched the stars fade and the night turn ruddy to the east. He explored his sensations of broken ribs and bruised spine. There was a great deal of pain. It would fade in time—three or four days, maybe—as everything healed, but right now the pain was fierce. He chewed on the end of his cold stogie and considered that pain was the human's friend; it taught lessons, if one embraced it as a hard taskmaster. But one could learn from such lessons, and Lawson intended not to let them go unheeded.

He did not wish to die in this half-life, in this half-world between vampires and humanity. The sunlight was harsher to them than to he, so…yes…they would be hiding somewhere near, and likely had already begun preparations for their daytime sleep.

Soon he was going to have to decide what to do. Time advanced; the sun was coming up as a scarlet fireball through the cypress trees and weeping willows. He felt its early heat in the still and steamy air. He felt its power prickling his skin. In another hour or so it would be as if the fiery hand of God was pressed against him. He was going to have to find some shelter, if he had to crawl into the church's belltower and curl up there around his broken ribs.

The night fled, and the sun strengthened.

The noise of the swamp became a harsher buzzing, as armies of insects reacted to the growing light and heat. Lawson crawled to the edge of the roof, moving painfully and slowly, and leaned over. There was a glassless window a few feet down. The sunlight was getting yellow now, the glare off the green water burning his eyes. He was going to have to turn himself into the correct position and get his boots on that window ledge, then lower his body through. The pain in his back and ribs were robbing both his strength and his power of will. The sun was hot, adding to his pain. His eyes were nearly blinded. It was going to be a hard descent, though only a matter of maybe four or five feet.

He was ready. He had to go now, before this pain worsened.

"Lawson! *Lawson!*"

He heard her voice, off somewhere to his left, and what remained of his heart leapt. Wherever she'd been hiding, she had heard the derringer shot too. He could barely see without the dark-tinted goggles. He shouted, "I'm here! Up on the steeple!"

There was a moment's pause. Then: "I see you!" He squinted against the glare and could make her out also. Ann was rowing a skiff up underneath him, and she looked to be covered with gray mud.

"Can you get down from there?" she called. "Can you jump?"

"Maybe," he said. It was thirty feet and would be a painful landing for him, even in the water. "Here! I'm going to drop this!" With an effort he removed his coat and waistcoat and got the leather harness and the sticks of dynamite off, lifting it over his head. "Get underneath it so it doesn't get wet. You ready?"

"I am."

Lawson dropped the harness over and it landed in the boat. "Matches, too. In the waistcoat pocket on the right. Have to keep those dry." He folded the waistcoat up and dropped it into the boat. He wished he had a rope to lower himself. Maybe there was one in the belltower, but the sun was burning him and his senses were going and he felt panic start to gnaw at him. He was going to have to jump, take the pain and get into that boat. Then find some shelter. He thought sure Ann would be dead by now. There was no time for further deliberation, he had to go.

Lawson gritted his teeth, got his body turned boots first and pushed himself off the roof.

It was bad, but the sunlight promised worse. He came up from the water and with Ann's help pulled himself over. He huddled in the boat, careful not to wet either the dynamite nor the waistcoat. "Shelter," he said hoarsely. "I'm burning."

Ann nodded and began to row toward the nearest half-submerged mansion, a structure with a partly-collapsed roof and green vines and moss covering its facade. "They came after me," she said, her face and hair coated with dried mud and mud freighting her clothes. Her voice was quiet and measured; it was the voice of a woman fighting shock. "Three of them. I swam. Got down in the mud. I stayed there as long as I could. Then I moved to another place. Down in the mud. I found a place I could hide. Lifted my face just a little above the water. Just a little. So I could breathe. They came after me, but I didn't move. For a long time. Then they went away. I saw them in their boats. Some left, but some stayed. They're hiding in these houses. My sister...they turned Eva into one of them, didn't they?"

"They did," said the vampire, who shivered as he burned.

"They're in these houses. All around us. Are they sleeping?"

"They are," said Lawson.

"Will they wake up in the daylight?"

"No. They're not like me. I can stand it…a little bit. Will you please hurry?"

"I will," she promised.

They glided into the cool shadows of the ruined mansion. Sunlight did stream through the windows, but there were trapped corners of velvet darkness. And in those corners were boats with bodies lying in them, wrapped up in protective material such as sailcloth, blankets and—as Lawson had used—window or bed curtains. In this one room alone there were four bodies lying in three boats, their skiffs tied one to another and anchored in place.

Lawson and Ann sat in their skiff in the green gloom, one battling his pain and the other fighting both her shock and grief.

The young woman's gloved fingers drew her pistol from her holster and began to load it with silver bullets from the ammo loops. Lawson's Colt with the rosewood grip, grimy with mud, was stuck down in her waistband. Her hands shook a little. "My gun's dried out," she said. "I cleaned it as best I could. Do you want me to kill them?"

"Yes," he answered.

"Do you want to see their faces before I do it? The woman…LaRouge. You don't want me to kill her, do you?"

"She won't be here," he said, relieved by the coolness and the shadows. "She knows Christian Melchoir is

dead. She suspects I'm still alive. So wherever she is…
she's somewhere else by now."

"You're not going to give up looking for her, are you?"

"Give up?" Lawson asked. He stared at the other
boats, and the sleepers. "No. I'm not ever giving up." He
saw one of the bodies twitch, as if enduring a bad dream.
Maybe they knew they were in danger; maybe they
would make an effort to rise from their sleep, even as the
bullets were delivered. But today belonged to the angels.

"I'm sorry about your sister," he said. "I'm sorry she
was caught up in this. I'm sorry…for everything." Even as
he spoke, he smelled the fragrance of Ann's warm blood.
He figured the sleepers did too, and they dreamed of
sinking their fangs deep and drinking their fill. Maybe
he might dream that of Ann, too. Maybe he was more
vampire than he wished. Maybe.

Maybe.

"After you finish with the bullets," Lawson said,
"there's the dynamite. I think Nocturne should be
returned to the swamp. What do you say?"

"I say…" Her fierce black eyes in the mud-covered
face peered at him. "I want to find my sister, and if she's
anything like *them*…I want to set her free. I can't bear
the thought of my Eva…like *that*. But no one will believe
us, will they?"

"Not many, but a few will."

"Where will you start looking for LaRouge?"

"I think they've overtaken another town at the edge of the swamp. I'll find it. That's where I'll start."

Ann set the six-shooter in her lap. She chewed on her bottom lip, as some of the bodies writhed in their shrouds.

"It seems to me," she said quietly, "that you need somebody to help you."

"I wouldn't ask anyone on this earth to do that. Not knowing what's out there waiting."

"It seems to me," Ann went on, "that you need somebody who can travel by day." Lawson was silent.

He thought the young woman had lost her mind. That this experience with the Dark Society had done her in. That she was deep in shock and had confused a challenge with a walk into the world of nightmares.

"I can't go back to what I was," she said, and as she stared at him two tears ran down through the dried mud on her cheeks. It was the sadness of loss, Lawson thought. It was the sadness of knowing what evil could do. "You know that. Nothing can be the same for me, ever again." She lifted the pistol. "I can shoot. I can fight. I can avenge my sister. Will you let me help you?" It was night work, Lawson thought. It all came down to night work, except…today was different. Today the sunrise had brought him something new. He didn't know how much to trust himself with Ann. He was still clinging to humanity, yes, but the vampirism was slowly overtaking him...and the need for human blood was getting stronger.

I travel by night, he thought. Yet it was true...he could use someone who could walk freely in the daytime world. With Ann, he might stand a greater chance of finding LaRouge, drinking her ichor and becoming fully human once more...if that was even possible, and not just a myth given to him by a legless Confederate corporal.

Lawson needed rest. He needed to take the shroud of one of these vampires after they'd been reduced to dust, wrap himself up as if in the wings of a darktime creature and sleep. He and Ann could start moving in the twilight, when his pain was lessened and his resolve firmed.

He felt he had many miles to go in this quest. He felt he had to endure many more horrors, many more trials and tribulations to fight what had been thrust upon him. He was sure Father Deale would like to meet Ann Kingsley. And if the future was uncertain, at least Lawson would know he had another gun on his side.

Ann was waiting for a reply, in this chamber that held equal measures of light and dark just as did life itself.

Lawson wished he had a cigar. He would buy a box of them, once he got back to New Orleans, and in the next few days after his bones had healed and his bruises were gone he would sit on a roof and ponder the stars, and count himself lucky to be alive even in this world where the Dark Society thrived.

Ann was waiting for a reply.

Lawson had taken many chances and trusted much to Fate. He decided to take one more chance, and trust to Fate now more than ever. The vampire gunslinger spoke.

The word he said, both gratefully and sadly for he knew what terrors awaited them, was: "Yes."